CHASING TIME

THOMAS REILLY

This is a work of fiction. Names, characters, places, and incidents are products of the author's imagination or are used fictitiously and are not to be construed as real. Any resemblance to actual events, locations, organizations, or persons, living or dead, is entirely coincidental.

World Castle Publishing, LLC
Pensacola, Florida

Paperback ISBN: 9781955086806
eBook ISBN: 9781955086813
First Edition World Castle Publishing, LLC, September 13, 2021
http://www.worldcastlepublishing.com

Cover: Karen Fuller
Editor: Maxine Bringenberg

PROLOGUE
ROME, AD 52

Lucius Fabius Antonius fixed his gaze across the room at the rectangular strongbox in his atrium and silently prayed to the gods for a miracle. A locking wooden chest, reinforced with iron and brass fittings and richly carved with images of Minerva, the Roman goddess of commerce, it sat securely anchored on a stone base. At this early hour, the intricately designed chest reflected the golden light of dawn pouring through the large, square opening of the roof.

Lucius's silent musings were suddenly shattered by the shrill voice of his wife, Appia, and he braced himself for another tirade.

"Lucius, it's just past the dawn hour, and I can already hear the merchants across the street setting up their stalls. I'm so tired of this domus. It might have served us well when we first moved here from that shabby apartment, but that was over five years ago. How do you expect me to entertain guests who are accustomed to the grandest villas? Our situation is simply embarrassing."

Lucius paused to collect himself before responding. "Appia, please be patient. You know I am working to remedy our condition. If the gods see fit, we should be able to move to that villa in the hills very soon. Now leave me, as I have some business to attend to."

In fact, the domus of Lucius was considered modest by the standards of the time and certainly by the standards of Appia. The single-story stone home sat across the street from the bustling tabernae, or stalls where merchants peddled their various wares of pottery, dishes, silks, spices, and other imported goods. Its main entrance was a large wooden door with prominent brass doorknobs. Beyond the door was a short vestibulum or hallway that led to the central atrium, an open central court where Lucius and Appia would typically greet their guests. No second courtyard, or peristylum, was present, nor was there any indoor pond. The rooms adjoining the atrium, although brightly decorated in florid colors, were small and lacked the grand mosaic floors constructed by master craftsmen that were common in the domi of Lucius and Appia's friends. Lucius's trade as an olive oil merchant in one of those very stalls across from his domus had been depressed as of late—the worst in eight years since the infamous economic depression of A.D. 44. This slowdown did not in any way quell the nearly daily protests from Appia about the humble state of their household.

Lucius was not born to upper class citizenry; indeed, successful Roman merchants rarely came from that echelon. Many traditional patrician families still considered careers as merchants to be demeaning. However, over the past ten years, he had built a successful, if somewhat vacillating trade in selling olive oil imported from southern Iberia. One important characteristic that greatly contributed to his success was his obsession with time, and in particular, his uncanny ability to predict future events. From his years as a young boy to the present, he had utilized this forecasting talent to his advantage. This ability manifested itself in many ways. For example, as a child, he had amazed his friends and augmented his popularity with them through his knack of predicting when certain boys would win at the various games of chance they played, especially those involving dice. As a young man, he had foreseen the exact date of a trading vessel's return to its home port after an almost year long voyage to the far reaches of India. This had enabled Lucius to seize the opportunity to purchase most of the ship's cargo of rare spices before other local merchants could act. The profit he had earned in selling those spices had enabled him to establish his olive oil enterprise.

Lucius's stare returned to the strongbox with its delicately crafted lock, and he wondered if somehow his unique talent could rescue him from his dire situation. For ironically, the very chest that he had purchased in an effort to placate Appia's aspirations and impress visitors now held the instrument of his downfall. Stored within the strongbox's confines, along with a few precious gold and silver items, was a contract, scrolled on papyrus sheets and marked with the emblem of Valeri, a prominent mensarii, or banking, family on the Via Sacra. Spurred on by incessant complaints from Appia and by his own personal ambitions, seven months earlier, Lucius had procured a huge loan of five hundred thousand sesterces from House Valeri to fund a trading voyage to the olive-rich area of Hispania in the Iberian peninsula.

Lucius recoiled in trepidation as he recalled the onerous terms he had accepted following difficult negotiations with an unyielding mensarii, Attitus Regulus.

"Lucius Antonius, please recognize the risk in this undertaking. Your galley must first traverse the dangerous currents and pirate-infested waters of the Mare Nostrum (Mediterranean) and then navigate up the Baetis River to reach the olive-rich province of Betica. Assuming your vessel even makes it that far, you must then hope that both the supply and quality of the local olive crop is sufficient to fully stock your cargo holds with premium product. And from there, your galley must again navigate the Mare Nostrum to reach home port safely."

Lucius had countered, "But Attitus Regulus, you must surely appreciate my experience in the olive oil trade. In recent years, I have co-funded many successful journeys. And as you know, the sea route is routinely monitored by naval patrols to protect against marauding pirates. These factors must certainly be considered for reducing the risks of such an undertaking."

In response, Attitus simply shrugged as if Lucius's words had no more relevance than the musings of a young child. "We will accept an interest rate of twenty-four percent on the loan to compensate for the dangers of this sea voyage."

"But twenty-four percent is more than twice the standard rate. Surely we can agree on more just terms," intoned Lucius.

"This is our final rate; we will accept nothing less. And in these difficult times, we must insist on one other condition."

Lucius shuddered at hearing these last words. What else beyond the already exorbitant interest rate could this obstinate mensarii extract from me? he thought.

Attitus continued. "As you are probably aware, in these difficult days, the Republic has wisely chosen to suspend its sanction on contracts where the lender may gain rights over the debtor's property. At House Valeri, we have found it necessary to resort to such unpleasant agreements to protect our interests. We must therefore impose an additional stipulation to your contract. If you fail to repay the first installment of your loan, an amount of fifty-thousand sesterces, within six months of the starting date of your voyage, we have the right to claim ownership of your domus."

Lucius felt numb as the banker's words reeled in his mind. Then anger took over. "This is outrageous. Surely you can't impose such oppressive terms on me as if I am nothing more than a spurious merchant."

Responding in an unnerving, calm tone, the banker

replied. "We understand your frustration. Nevertheless, this is the way it must be. There is no other option unless, of course, you decide to reject our loan."

Despite his serious misgivings, Lucius eventually accepted the mensaii's onerous terms. Unfortunately, the difficult economy had forced his hand; there simply were no other practical options to secure the required funds. He reasoned that, as the sole financial backer of this expedition, he would capture the lion's share of profits on eventual sales of the imported olive oil rather than share them with other merchants as was his usual custom. With the expected windfall from this voyage, Lucius could finally put Appia's griping behind him by purchasing that grand villa she coveted in the hills of Rome. Of course, such a domus would also reflect his richly deserved status as a member of Rome's elite society.

Furthermore, he had convinced himself the risk of loan default was low. Based on his own trading experiences, he expected the voyage to be completed well before the six months, by which time profits from olive oil sales would be flooding into his treasury. Notably, however, his confidence did not extend to the level where he felt comfortable enough to confide with Appia about this last condition.

Unfortunately, over the past several weeks, stories from returning vessels about unusually fierce storms in the western seas had disquieted Lucius, and, indeed, the contract deadline was fast approaching with no sign of his vessel. In fact, the six-month deadline was tomorrow, the kalends or first day of Februarius, the traditional time of month for debtors to settle their debts. This unexpected delay and the consequences of a looming default were the reasons for Lucius's recent obsessions and sleepless nights. This morning he was planning to remove the chirographum, or handwritten contract, that represented the evidence for the agreed terms from its locked compartment in his strongbox and review it for what seemed like the hundredth time in vain hopes of discovering some unknown clause or passage that would alleviate his debt to House Valeri. He needed a miracle!

The bronze key to the strongbox's compartment lay dangling from a silver band around Lucius's index finger. Affluent Romans generally wore keys as rings on their fingers, not only to keep them handy but also to signal that the wearer was rich and important. Only the most prominent citizens had jewelry made of bronze, for central Italia itself was not rich in metal ores. Therefore, trade networks from various lands were required to meet the demand from Rome. As with olive oil, one important source was Iberia, perhaps Rome's richest province. Ever since its conquest during the Punic Wars, this territory, with its rich deposit of mineral ores, continued to provide Rome with a variety of metals, including the copper and tin that were forged together to form bronze.

As an olive oil merchant with an acquired knowledge of the commodity trading between Rome and the Iberian Peninsula, Lucius had occasionally procured small supplies of these precious metals for his own personal use. When commissioning one of the foremost smiths in the city to craft his strongbox, he had also provided the craftsman with small amounts of these rare metals and instructions to forge a key that properly reflected Lucius's prominence in the Roman hierarchy. In turn, the smith had created a true masterpiece, a bronze key ring featuring intricate geometric patterns and images. One end of Lucius's key was anchor-shaped and had notches carved into its tip that were designed to fit into the slit of the compartment's lock, lift the metal pin tumblers, and pull the lock's bolt to one side. The other end featured an easy-to-grasp bow with a hole where it was attached to a finger ring with a tiny metal clasp. The key's most prominent feature was its five-inch shaft. Unlike most keys of the time, whose shafts were very simple rods or crudely shaped animal forms, this one was exquisitely sculpted in the image of the Roman god Janus. Lucius had specifically requested this image because his obsession with time triggered a particular affinity towards Janus, the god of beginnings, transitions, and time. Janus was depicted as a two-faced image, representing both the past and the future. The small icon appeared almost lifelike to Lucius, complete with its penetrating eyes, flowing beards, and graceful, twisting torsos chiseled on both sides.

As Lucius looked down to grasp the key, he suddenly noticed small but piercing red beams of light emanating from one set of eyes. How they shined, like glowing embers, sparkling and dancing, in the ashen residue of a dying fire! This was odd; he'd never noticed such light discharges before.

He then recalled the words from the smith who had forged the implement. "Never has such a bellowing flame been crafted as in the forging of this key of bronze; it was as if Janus himself was directing my efforts." Lucius had dismissed the man's words at the time, but now he pondered them. Could there be some divine magic behind this key?

Lucius momentarily dismissed his thought as the red lights dissipated. He removed the key from his finger, inserted it into the lock slot of the compartment on the strongbox, and turned it to unlock the bolt. Removing the chirographum, he began to study the contract in detail. After so many reviews, Lucius had most of the clauses and dates committed to memory. Therefore, he was astonished when he came to the last page of the agreement, for he noticed a new heading and text, words he had not seen before. Under the title of Contractus, it read as follows: On this day, the Kalends of Februarius, the Argentarii Guild hereby renders payment of fifty-thousand sesterces to citizen Lucius Maximus Antonius.

How had these words materialized on his contract? Except

for his own intrusions, the compartment was always locked, and he carried the only key. In fact, he had examined the contract just yesterday, and he knew that no such words were included. Yet here they were, staring him in the face. How could this be?

In studying the new text, Lucius realized the contract referenced a future date, tomorrow, the kalends of Februarius. Recalling the strange lights emanating from his key moments earlier, he wondered if this was a sign of some divine intervention by Janus. If so, was this message offering him a path forward to save his estate from the onerous terms of the Valeri bank loan? He knew he had to act on this information.

The new contract referenced the Argentarii Guild, a league of bankers Lucius knew only by reputation. Argentarii were private citizens who managed money and mercantile transactions, not in the service of the Republic, but in the interest of their own tabernae. This contrasted with the role of the mensarii such as Valeri, who were public bankers conducting business in service of the state. In spite of the burdensome terms he had negotiated with Valeri, Lucius had purposely rejected any dealings with the argentarii because so many of their members were unscrupulous and dangerous. Furthermore, several of Lucius's colleagues who had dealings with them spoke of the argentarii with contempt. However, his situation was now critical, and Lucius rationalized these desperate times required desperate measures. He knew that many argentarii conducted their business in shops in and around the area by the Janus Geminus shrine, which was a small arch dedicated nearly three centuries earlier in honor of Janus. This additional connection with the god of time did not escape Lucius.

Calling for his slaves to prepare his litter, he was carried through the muck of the crowded city streets to the northeast part of the city where the shrine was located. As he approached the temple, he studied it closely. It was a small rectangular structure with two brass doors opposite each other; these doors were arched to join at the top and flanked by two columns. By tradition, its two doors were opened to indicate that Rome was at war and closed during times of peace. Carved into one niche on the right-hand door was a bronze statue of Janus with his right hand extended and grasping a golden key. Lucius couldn't help but think of his own Janus key and shuddered in apprehension as he remembered the piercing red beams of light that had emanated from its eyes. Congregating under the arch that provided cover from the intense, mid-day sun, he noticed several argentarii conducting their business.

As Lucius descended from his litter, a small, elderly man with a furrowed, weather-beaten face appeared mysteriously, almost like an apparition emerging out of the blinding sunlight. As the old codger opened his mouth to speak, Lucius noticed two rows of yellowed, pointed teeth that reminded him of the spinous canines in wild dogs that roamed the poorer sections of Roma.

"What is your business?" the stranger asked Lucius.

"What do you mean?" replied Lucius warily.

"I mean, what is your trade?"

"I am an importer and seller of the finest Iberian olive oil."

"Ah," answered the stranger. "Iberian olive oil, truly a precious commodity. Let me assist you with your dilemma. For a small portion of your oil shipment that will arrive shortly, I will pay you fifty thousand sesterces to alleviate your debt obligation. Meet me here tomorrow morning, and we will finalize our agreement."

Lucius stared at the man in astonishment. How could he know the exact terms of Lucius's first payment to Valeri? Also, Lucius was struck by the stranger's prediction that his hoped-for oil shipment from the Iberian peninsula would be arriving shortly. How could the banker know if Lucius's ship would even reach port safely? Lucius's first impulse was to reject this man's proposal; it seemed too mysterious to be legitimate. But then he recalled the strange events of the day with the mysterious Janus key and his premonition that it was meant to provide a solution to his problems. He agreed to the follow-up meeting.

Lucius returned home and immediately pulled out the chirographum from his strongbox. Just as mysteriously as the text describing his transaction with the argentarii had appeared, now the words had vanished. Truly some mysterious force was at work.

The following morning, Lucius returned to the Janus Geminus shrine, where he met the stranger and completed their agreement. In return for the fifty-thousand sesterces that the man handed over, Lucius agreed to provide ten amphorae of olive oil, stone jars that held approximately seventy liters each. By all mercantile standards, these were extremely favorable terms for Lucius. He then had himself carted to the Via Sacra, home of House Valeri, where he paid the first installment of his obligation, fifty-thousand sesterces.

TWO WEEKS LATER, PORT OF OSTIA

The city of Ostia was the principal commercial port for Rome. Daily, its citizens would watch ocean-going craft from across the Mediterranean dock at wooden piers, unload precious cargo, and transfer their payload to barges for the final twenty-mile transit up the Tiber River to Rome. This day, clear and sunny, many viewers noticed a ship bearing the flag of House Antonius on its mast entering the port. The vessel's keel sank low in the water, indicating it was fully loaded with important cargo of some sort. In fact, the ship was laden with virgin olive oil from Iberia.

CHAPTER ONE

April 1, 1965

Anthony Lucas, known as Tony to his friends, squirmed in the seat of his eighth-grade classroom as he waited anxiously for the school day to end. As usual, his obsession with time had led him to play a favorite mental game, predicting the exact time remaining until the 3:00 p.m. dismissal bell sounded. Sixteen minutes after two o'clock, he noted to himself and then confirmed his prognostication by turning to witness the second hand slowly sweep past three on the large clock hanging on the front left wall, indicating a time of exactly 2:16 p.m. Forty-four minutes to go.

It had been a curious school day at St. Bridget's Grammar School in the Bay Ridge section of Brooklyn. This was the occasion the entire school had been anticipating for several weeks, the date when, finally, the sixty-year-old time capsule would be opened and its contents revealed. The student assembly had been abuzz since last month when construction of a new gymnasium had unearthed a small copper box buried under the cornerstone of the original red-brick school building. Various rumors, ranging from plausible to fantastical, had circulated about the box's contents. Tony's personal favorite, which had been started by his friend, Joe Hubbard, suggested that the box contained the brains of an unidentified body that had been discovered several months ago in an abandoned building, just a mile or so from their school. A few days later, St. Bridget's principal, Sister Mary Stella, had put an end to most of the wild speculations with an announcement over the school's loudspeaker that the box was, in fact, a time capsule, buried there by the first graduating class of St. Bridget's sixty years ago, in 1905. Furthermore, the school would celebrate the capsule's discovery by holding an opening ceremony on April first of this year, exactly sixty years since its burial.

Earlier that day, Tony, along with the entire student body, had assembled in the large auditorium for the ceremony where Mr. Cato, a prominent parishioner of St. Bridget's and whose local grocery store was the principal sponsor of the school's little league baseball teams, had strolled onto the stage carrying the rusted, soldered, copper box. Approximately two feet long and one foot wide, it was not very remarkable in appearance. As the students watched in amazement, Mr. Cato attacked the box with a vigor that seemed more appropriate for a construction worker wielding his hammer drill than a mild-mannered store owner. The din from the pounding and sawing with hammer, chisel, and hacksaw reverberated throughout the auditorium until the lid was successfully removed.

Now was the moment of revelation; Tony silently hoped Mr. Cato would uncover something really surprising inside. Slowly he pulled out the first item, a yellowed piece of crumbling newspaper. Sister Stella, who shared the stage with Mr. Cato, immediately assumed the role of narrator and announced in a booming voice that seemed totally incongruous with her small, delicate physique that it was part of the front page of The New York Times from April 1, 1905. This two-person act was repeated as Mr. Cato drew item after item from the box with Sister Stella providing a short narrative description: stamps, coins, an old black and white photograph of President Theodore Roosevelt, colored marbles, a pocket knife, a list of signatures from the 1905 eight grade class of St. Bridget's until the box was empty. Nothing earth-shattering there thought Tony, feeling a bit deflated after all the earlier excitement the box had generated. Sister Stella brought the ceremony to its conclusion by announcing that one lucky member of the eighth grade would be chosen that afternoon to take the box and its contents home for the night and share them with his or her family, after which the items would be returned to school for display here in the auditorium.

Back in his classroom, Tony's thoughts had already returned to his beloved Yankees and their upcoming baseball season, which was set to start in a few weeks. He snapped to attention when his teacher, Sister Constantia, asked that everyone write their name on a piece of paper and submit it for a drawing to determine the lucky student who would win the privilege of taking the time capsule and its contents home for the night. Tony passively completed this task and waited while Sister Constantia collected the papers, placed them in a cardboard box, and drew out one crumpled piece. "Anthony Lucas," she called out.

Tony's first reaction was surprise; he had never won any important contest in his life. He then remembered that the prize was somewhat underwhelming; why couldn't the award be something nifty like a new car, a trip to Europe, or almost anything else? Nevertheless, he sheepishly acknowledged the applause of his classmates.

Upon the sounding of the dismissal bell, Tony ambled down to the auditorium to pick up the box and its contents and received a short, instructive lecture from Sister Stella about the proper care and treatment of the historic articles.

"Remember," she declared, "they are a symbol of our school's past; treat them with the respect they deserve."

"Yes, Sister."

By the time Tony exited the school building carrying his

bookbag with one arm and carefully cradling the copper box in his other, all his friends had disappeared. He started the six-block walk home and soon turned onto the busy Third Avenue thoroughfare with its commercial storefronts, businesses, and overhead apartments. He approached Louise's, his family's favorite Italian restaurant, where they often celebrated important occasions such as birthdays, graduations, and the like. Tony noticed a cluster of large, empty cardboard boxes in front of the restaurant, lined up in a row for pickup by the sanitation truck later that afternoon. Luigi's Virgin Olive Oil-Imported from Italy read the label on each box. In smaller print were the words: May contain up to 50% olive oil from Spain. *Wow,* thought Tony to himself; *they sure go through a lot of olive oil here.*

Tony continued walking past the restaurant when he noted a glint of sunshine reflecting off a point in the sidewalk between two of the cartons. Bending down to examine the source of the reflected light, he observed an old, rusted, metal ring attached to an ancient-looking key with notches cut into its tip. The most remarkable feature of the key was its shaft; it was approximately five inches in length and intricately carved in the figure of a two-faced, ancient-looking man. Picking the key up to study it in more detail, he noted a set of piercing, almost life-like eyes on each face staring back at him. *What a neat little souvenir,* thought Tony. He dropped it in his book bag and continued home.

CHAPTER TWO

The large, three-story, white-stucco colonial stood out from the neighboring homes on the block by nature of its large front yard, unusual for this section of Brooklyn where most fronts were matchbox sized. Tony raced through the stout, oaken front door, past the narrow entranceway, and into the spacious living room whose floors were lined with authentic oriental rugs that were his mother's pride and joy. Tony always enjoyed coming home; he viewed it as his safe and happy environment.

In an excited voice, he yelled out, "I'm home; guess what I won!"

As his mother joined his older sister Karen to greet him, she replied, "My gracious, what's so exciting?"

"I won this," he said, pointing to the rusty copper box. "Well, I didn't exactly win it. But I won the drawing at school to take it home and examine the contents with you guys. It's a time capsule with stuff from the first class of St. Bridget's in 1905. I have it for the night. Then I have to return it to school tomorrow."

"How wonderful!" his mother exclaimed. "Let's look at them tonight when your father returns from his calls."

Tony's dad was a pediatrician who spent Thursday afternoons attending rounds at the local hospital and then driving all over Brooklyn until late evening, making house call visits to his sick patients. Following his dad's return home a few hours later and a delicious pot roast dinner, the family assembled around the copper box, prominently displayed in the center of the living room coffee table. Despite their sixty-year-old age, most of the memorabilia in the box were well-preserved, and the family spent several minutes removing and examining the various items. The exception was the yellowed, partial front page of the April 1, 1905, New York Times. Most of the bottom half of the paper had withered away, probably due to a bit of moisture that had infiltrated the box. Eventually, Tony's dad carefully cradled the ancient newspaper page in his steady physician hands and spoke.

"Tony, this is amazing. You are providing us with an authentic piece of American history. Listen to these headlines from sixty years ago: '$12,600,000 Discrepancy in Gas Company's Bonds'; 'Alfred G. Vanderbilt Arrested for Speeding'; 'H.H. Rogers Defends Rockefeller's Methods'; and 'Robbed Senator's House-Mr. Burrows of Michigan.'"

Tony asked his father. "Dad, those stories hardly seem like the kind of news that make headlines. No stories about foreign countries or world events. What's the big deal with speeding, robbing, or company bonds? That kind of stuff belongs buried inside the paper, not on the front page."

Mrs. Lucas interjected. "Tony, Karen, you have to realize that back then, America was a much different country than it is today. News stories from that era tended to be much more provincial, reflecting America's relative isolation from most world affairs. It wasn't until World War I ended in 1918 that America started to emerge as a major player on the world stage."

Karen then asked. "I know a Rockefeller is the governor of New York. Does this headline refer to the same family? And who were the Vanderbilts?"

Dr. Lucas answered his daughter. "The Vanderbilts and

the Rockefellers were titans of American industry in the early twentieth century, specifically in railroads and oil. Any stories about those families attracted considerable attention from the general public. They were like the rock stars of their day. Our governor, Nelson Rockefeller, is the grandson of John D. Rockefeller, the founder of the huge oil empire."

The Lucas family spent the next several minutes discussing the contents that had survived sixty years in a metal box and reflected on life for the average person at a time with few phones and cars and no television or computers. Finally, Tony's parents agreed that this had been an excellent and educational evening, thanked Tony for sharing his success with the entire family, and sent the kids off to bed.

In his bedroom, Tony was changing out of his clothes into his pajamas when he remembered the key he had stored in his book bag. Retrieving the small icon, he marveled at its intricately carved details and wondered about its history. *It seems so old,* he thought. *I bet there are some interesting stories behind it.* Promising to share his discovery with his friends and family in the morning, he dropped the key into the opened copper box that was lying on the floor next to him, replaced its lid, and hopped into his bed.

Tony awoke promptly at six-forty-five the next morning. He continuously surprised his parents with his uncanny ability to anticipate the hour and wake up, unaided by any alarm, in time for any occasion or event, such as a 6:00 a.m. mass where he had been assigned to serve as an altar boy at St. Bridget's Church. He just had a special sense about time, whether it was predicting it, anticipating it, or making the best use of it. His parents often joked that he had a passion for time.

Rushing to complete his pre-school routine of a quick hot shower, a breakfast of frosted flakes and milk, and a goodbye hug to his father as he headed off for his early hospital rounds, Tony headed back to his room for last-minute preparations. Squinting his eyes at the sunshine streaming through the window as he peeked at the outdoor thermometer, he noted an unseasonable temperature of 68° F. That's great, he thought. It's warm enough to wear my Yankees jacket today. He threw open his closet door and started rummaging through the hanging garments until he located the lightweight jacket among the jumble of tangled jerseys, sweatshirts, and pants. Tony grabbed the jacket and put it on.

Bending down to retrieve the rusted copper box containing the old artifacts, he suddenly remembered the ancient-looking key from last night. Removing the lid to retrieve the key, he recoiled in utter surprise as his gaze was met by two piercing red beams of lights emanating from one set of eyes on the two-faced icon. Transfixed by the penetrating stare from the icon's face, illuminated to almost lifelike form by the beaming lights, Tony actually wondered if the old man was trying to communicate a message to him. Recovering from his momentary shock, he nervously cradled the key in his right hand and tried to locate any on/off switch or small battery compartment that might be the power source of the emanating lights. He found none. *How strange!*

Recovering from the startling episode, Tony stashed the key in his jacket pocket and examined the contents of the box to assure all was in order before returning them to school. Taking a moment to gently remove the yellowed, tattered newspaper page and read it for himself, he received his second, jolting surprise of the morning. The date printed on the top line read, April 1, 2025.

Wait a second, he thought. *Yesterday the date read April 1, 1905. Today the paper is dated sixty years in the future instead of sixty years in the past! How can that be?*

He then turned to read the headlines his father had recited to them last evening and again was astonished to discover none of the headings were the same. Rather, they referred to stories about events or people that were alien to him. One headline read, "Former U.S. President Bill Clinton Appointed as Special Envoy to Sudan." *Bill Clinton?* questioned Tony as he quickly scanned the few lines of the story that were still visible in the remaining top half of the newspaper page. They briefly described the long career of the forty-second United States president, William Jefferson Clinton. Tony quietly recited to himself the last few presidents he had studied in American history. *Let's see, there was FDR, then Truman, and Eisenhower, followed by Kennedy, and now LBJ. I never heard of a President Clinton,* he thought. *The only Clinton I know is Robby Clinton from my class.*

A second headline turned to a more familiar subject but again seemed strange and futuristic. "Yankees Look to Rebound from Last Year's Disappointing Season." What particularly caught Tony's eye in the ensuing story was a reference to the worst collapse in Yankee history since their momentous fall from grace in the 1965 season. 1965 season? That was this year, and the season hadn't even started yet. And how could the perennial powerhouse Yankees, who had won the last five American League pennants in a row with their formidable lineup of Mantle, Maris, Howard, and the rest, fall from grace this year? The team had unfinished business to attend to after last October's disappointing loss to the St. Louis Cardinals in the seventh game of the World Series.

The strangest headline read like science fiction to Tony. "Miracle Cure for Crippling Disease." Most of the few remaining lines in the underlying story were unrecognizable smudges of ink. The few words that Tony could decipher included pioneering, discovery, and the name George Janusowski. Tony had no way of determining if that name represented a patient, a doctor, a discoverer of the cure, or someone else associated with this story. In addition to these few words, Tony could also make out short snippets of letters that made no sense to him: "BMAA-in..." and

"Almed." Tony rubbed his eyes in confusion. The whole thing was too strange; what was he looking at?

CHAPTER THREE

Tony's thoughts turned back to reality when he heard his mother's voice calling from downstairs. "Hurry up, Tony, or you'll be late for school."

He replaced the newspaper in the copper box, positioned its cover in place, and grabbed the box and his schoolbag. Rushing downstairs, he yelled goodbye to his mother as he sprinted out the front door. After one block, he rendezvoused with his friend Kevin Maynard, and they continued the trek to school together.

"Kevin," he cried out in an excited tone. "You'll never believe this. I found a magic key yesterday that changed the headlines on that old newspaper from the time capsule. They now read about events sixty years in the future instead of sixty years in the past. It's kind of unbelievable."

Kevin looked at his friend as if he were an alien visitor from Mars. "Tony, you may be good at predicting some things, but this story proves you're crazy."

"Then look at this." Tony reached his hand into the jacket pocket to grab the key. However, all his fingers clasped was empty air. Darn it, he thought. It's that hole from last year that I forgot to ask Mom to fix. Unfortunately, the key must have fallen out of his pocket during their walk to school. With the distant clamor of the school bell signaling for students to report to their classrooms, Tony had no chance to retrace his steps to find the key; he would have to search for it on his way home later that day. "Wait until you see the headlines on the old newspaper," Tony said to Kevin as they hurried towards the school.

From his classroom, Tony was sent down to the principal's office to return the copper box and its historic contents. While there, the administrative assistant, Mrs. Dombrowski, took the box from Tony and told him the items would be displayed in the auditorium for all the students to view. Tony started to explain his story of the changing headlines to her, but she gave him such a stern look that he stopped talking and cowered back to his classroom.

Later that morning, it was time for Sister Constantia's class to visit the auditorium and view the items. Tony turned to Kevin and said, "Now you'll see what I mean."

As they entered the large room, Tony noticed that all the items had been removed from the box and placed atop a long table on the auditorium's stage. The students formed a line and started a slow, single-file procession so that everyone had a chance to observe each piece closely. Moving along the line, Tony noted that none of the students ahead of him appeared surprised when they examined the single newspaper page. *Are they looking at it closely enough?* he thought. When he reached the newspaper, the mystery was solved. The date on the top of the page read, April 1, 1905, and the headlines and short narratives described the same 1905 events that his family had discussed last evening. Everything had changed back! How was this possible? *Did I just dream about the futuristic headlines and stories this morning? No,* he thought. *I was as wide awake this morning as I am now.* To add insult to his injured state of mind, his friend Kevin whispered to him, "Since when is 1905 the future?"

Tony waited anxiously for the school day to end so he could search for the key. Following the normal three o'clock dismissal, he slowly made his way home, focusing his eyes on the ground and carefully retracing, in reverse, the route he had used that morning. To taunts from his schoolmates of, "Hey slowpoke, what are you looking for?" he scoured the sidewalk for the missing key. No luck; it was lost as mysteriously as it had been found. When Tony finally arrived home, he decided it was best to put the entire affair behind him; better to pretend the incident never happened than to risk the scorn of his friends and family by relating far-fetched stories of mysterious keys and future events.

CHAPTER FOUR

September 1, 1965

"Breakfast is ready, Tony. Put down that paper and come and eat."

"Okay, Mom."

As Tony scarfed down a plate of scrambled eggs, bacon, and toast, he reflected on his summer vacation that was drawing to a close. *What a great few months; why does it have to end?* His summer had included many trips to the beach at Breezy Point, a gated community located on the far western end of the Rockaway Peninsula in Queens. Dr. and Mrs. Lucas's best friends owned a small bungalow in the predominantly blue-collar, Irish Catholic community and had provided them with a season's pass. Tony loved riding the crest of the huge waves on his fiberglass boogieboard and walking along the expansive shoreline with the Manhattan skyline shimmering in the distance. Tony's dad often stated that Breezy Point was a piece of the New York City landscape that most people wouldn't recognize.

Tony also reminisced about the many trips he had taken to the New York World's Fair, the large international exhibit at Flushing Meadows in Queens, which would be closing its gates in a few months. Tony's mom had permitted his older sister Karen and him to travel to the fairgrounds by themselves, and they had often hopped on the subway in Bay Ridge and transferred to the 7 line that ran to Flushing Meadows. Tony loved strolling through the fairgrounds, visiting the pavilions of foreign countries, and sampling the incredible food, such as Belgian waffles slathered with whipped cream and strawberries. However, the most interesting features of the fair for Tony were the exhibitions that emphasized time; either displays of past eras in human history or attractions that offered predictions of life sixty years into the future, including astronauts who could live for months in space stations orbiting the earth, video phones that allowed callers to see each other, and robots that would carry out household tasks. *What a fantastic future in store for us if any of these predictions come to pass,* he thought.

Returning his focus to the sports pages of his newspaper, he noticed the headline announcing another Yankee loss. *Who would have thought the great Yankees would be playing sub-five hundred ball and trailing five other teams at this late point in the season?* He suddenly recalled the mysterious, altered story from the time capsule last May, referencing the worst Yankee collapse since the 1965 season. *Could there really be some truth to those strange stories from the 2025 front page?* Just in case, Tony decided it would be a good idea to write down everything he could remember about them before he forgot the details. He ran to his room, grabbed a pen and piece of loose-leaf paper from his desk drawer, and started to print out his memories in large block letters. *Let me see,* he thought; *the date on the newspaper was April 1, 2025, and the first story mentioned the appointment of a former president to Sudan—what was his name?* He recalled that the man shared a last name with his former classmate Robby Clinton; *that's right, not Robby but Bill, Bill Clinton.* Next, Tony scribbled some notes on the Yankee story he remembered, that the team hoped to rebound from their worst collapse since the 1965 season.

Finally, he tried to recollect details about the last story he had seen that day. He remembered that only a few words had been legible under the headline banner proclaiming a miracle cure for a crippling disease. *Let me think; there was a discovery and some Polish-sounding man's name.* George Janusowski suddenly rolled off his tongue. Tony thought the name had a certain ring to it; that's probably why he remembered it so readily.

Another thought was gnawing in the back of Tony's mind; he knew that a few clusters of letters or acronyms had also appeared in print. One grouping he suddenly recalled was almed; what was the other? As he was contemplating this puzzle, he noticed a small ticket stub on his desk, a souvenir from a recent concert his family had attended at the Brooklyn Music Academy. To his surprise, Tony had enjoyed hearing Beethoven's Seventh Symphony that evening. He remembered thinking, How can anyone write music for so many different instruments?

However, now the bold initials of BMA on the stub, the abbreviation of the venue for that evening's concert, triggered a reaction in his mind. BMA; that was it! The last grouping of letters from that article was BMAA-in.

Tony rapidly recorded the letters on the sheet of paper, folded it in half, and, reaching for the bookshelf, grabbed the small metal safe that served as the repository for his most treasured items. After entering the combination of nineteen and five for the simple, two-wheel locking mechanism, he opened the safe door, placed the folded sheet of paper inside, closed the safe, and turned the tumbler to lock it. He probably would never need to review these notes, but one never knew.

CHAPTER FIVE

Tony sat cross-legged on his bed while listening to the pulsating sounds of the Beatles emanating from his small transistor radio. The station was playing "Help," his favorite song by the superstar quartet. *Funny,* he thought. *I never really paid attention to the words before, but that line "Help me if you can I'm feeling down" really sums up how I feel about high school.* With the Labor Day weekend marking the official end of summer, Tony prepared for his first day of high school with a fair amount of anxiety.

After eight years in the confined locale of St. Bridget's single brick building, he felt ready for some type of change. But was he truly prepared to enter the vast dominion of Alexander Hamilton High School in Brooklyn? The school sat on a ten-acre campus and was divided into three separate buildings, one containing most of the classrooms, the library, cafeteria, and administrative offices, a second featuring a modern science center with laboratory facilities for biology, chemistry, and physics, and a third comprising a full-sized gymnasium. Spread over the grounds were a quarter-mile cinder track, baseball and football fields, four hard-surface tennis courts, and an oversized parking lot. The entire venue seemed more like a small city than a school to Tony.

It didn't take long for Tony to recognize that the extent of its demographic diversity matched the school's physical size. Unlike St. Bridget's, where the student body was primarily composed of kids from Catholic, middle-class families, Hamilton High encompassed a heterogeneous group of students representing different races, religions, and social backgrounds.

As Tony spent his first few days cautiously circulating from class to class and familiarizing himself with his new routine and surroundings, the combination of novelty, numbers, and acreage literally overwhelmed him. Hugging the walls as he plodded from classroom to classroom among the bustling throngs of students, Tony readily melted into the background. In classes, he positioned himself in the rear of every room in hopes of avoiding any scrutiny or attention. Having a sidekick to navigate the strange new surroundings would have eased his transition; however, none of his best friends from St. Bridget's had joined him at Hamilton High, and his natural shyness hindered his ability to make new friends.

Tony had yet to experience a teenage growth spurt and was one of the shortest kids in the entire school body. His stature made him easy prey for the many bullies he encountered in the hallways and grounds of the school and added to his overall anxiety.

Lunchtime was particularly challenging, and finding a place to sit was a nightmare. During one fateful lunch period, Tony spent endless minutes circulating the cafeteria floor in desperate search of an empty seat and finally located an unoccupied chair at one of the long, rectangular tables. Fretting to himself, he thought, I would rather be anywhere in the world than here. As he sat down, bowing his head to avoid eye contact with any of the other students, he sensed rather than viewed a pair of dark, intimidating eyes boring in on him. Slowly raising his head to face this looming threat, his vision centered on a brutish, dark-haired boy with a crooked smile and a pockmarked complexion sitting on the opposite side of the table.

Apparently, the leader of this particular faction of students, he sternly challenged Tony from the opposite side of the table. "What do you think you're doing?"

"Um, having my lunch."

"Not here, you ain't."

Before Tony could utter a response, this titan, approximately twice Tony's size and more suited to pounding opponents into submission in boxing matches than attending ninth-grade classes, snatched Tony's lunch bag out of his hand and proceeded to gulp down the ham and cheese sandwich tenderly prepared that morning by his mother. Between giant-sized bites, the bully menaced, "If I ever see you here again, it won't be your sandwich I will make disappear. This is my table, and don't even think about sitting here again."

Tony glanced around the table for some sympathetic support, but all he noted was a series of hardened faces staring at him with unequivocal contempt. He quickly rose and sheepishly left the cafeteria, so much for today's lunch.

Unfortunately for Tony, this particular ruffian, who coincidentally was also named Anthony, was a student in Tony's algebra class, and barely a day had elapsed when he didn't pull some particular stunt, such as emptying Tony's school bag contents on the floor or heckling him with demeaning and curse-filled taunts, all designed to make Tony's existence miserable.

Throughout this difficult period, Tony's rock was his mother. He loved both parents; however, his father's hectic and bustling schedule dictated that his mom was the usual go-to parent for any personal issues or problems. Consequently, Tony turned to her whenever he needed advice, support, or just some old-fashioned, maternal comfort. This situation proved no different, and one afternoon after returning from another depressing day at school, he unloaded his burdens to her. "I didn't think high school would be so bad; I never knew there were so many mean people in the world."

Tony's mom hugged him and began to soothe his tattered feelings with her comforting and judicious words. "Tony, you are a very special person. Not only are you kind, smart, and tenacious in problem solving, but you have a unique talent for predicting things that I know will serve you well in life.

"But why did you send me to a place I hate?"

"Your father and I sent you to Hamilton High because we felt exposure to its large and diverse student population will prepare you for many of the experiences that life presents. Remember, we can't live our lives in a vacuum."

"I don't think I'll even make it out of high school."

"Don't think like that. Look at these difficult days as a challenge, and try to determine how you can use your talents to overcome obstacles and improve your situation. And remember, if things don't work out in a few more weeks, your father and I will take action to remedy the situation. But for now, it would be best if you try and find your own solutions."

Tony took his mother's words to heart and, reinvigorated by her advice, set out to map a new course for his high school journey.

A few days later, Tony slouched at his desk before algebra class, reviewing his open notebook while biting the tip of his pencil. *Quadratic equations – who is ever going to need this stuff?* he thought. Mr. Murphy, his mousey teacher who looked younger than many of his students, had scheduled a test for today, and many of Tony's classmates were nervously chattering about the upcoming exam. Over the din, Tony clearly discerned one thunderous voice echoing across the classroom; it was that of his personal nemesis as he proclaimed to no one in particular, "No way I'm ready for this exam today; I need more time to study."

Tony, who had just experienced another of his unique premonitions about the future, made a quick decision to himself and timidly spoke out, "I wouldn't worry about today's exam. I have a strong feeling that Mr. Murphy won't be in today, and the exam will be cancelled."

Glaring back with disdain written all over his face, Anthony retorted. "Who said you can talk? And that's crazy; do you think you're some kind of psychic or something?"

Stung by this harsh reprimand, Tony's face reddened, and he cowered back in his seat, wondering to himself why he had ever spoken up in the first place. However, a few minutes later, the school's principal, Mr. Hayes, strode into the room and called the class to attention. "I have an announcement to make," he started. "Mr. Murphy is out sick and informed me that the exam scheduled for today will be postponed until his return, probably in two more days. For now, you may use this time as a study period."

In response to these welcome words, the class exclaimed a resounding "Yes" in unison, and relieved by the postponement, opened their algebra books to review the subject material.

Later that day during lunch period, Tony was replaying his daily routine of searching for an empty seat when he heard a loud voice beckoning, "Hey kid, come over here. How did you know that Murphy was out today?"

Astonished, he looked over and saw that Anthony was talking to him. He warily approached the sitting giant and answered, "I just have a knack for time and for knowing that certain events will happen before they actually do. I can't explain it, but this morning I just knew that Mr. Murphy wouldn't show up."

Anthony regarded his classmate with a puzzled stare and then retorted, "You're okay, kid; come here and sit with us."

That one incident in algebra class where he displayed

his special talent proved to be the turning point in Tony's high school adventure. From then on, Anthony adopted him not only as a member of his inner circle but in time as a good friend. This, in turn, opened all types of opportunities for Tony as he grew in both confidence and stature.

Tony's unique gift also cemented his standings among his peers. One school assembly period even became part of the folklore of Hamilton High. At a pep rally for their football team, whose game against arch-rival Lincoln High was scheduled for the upcoming Saturday, Tony joined the loud and raucous crowd in cheering each player as they were introduced. Following the player salutes, the student emcee asked everyone to write their name and score prediction on a piece of paper, fold it in the shape of an airplane, and aim it for a large bin sitting in the center of the gym floor. The student body became engrossed in the contest, and before long, the air was filled with fluttering paper planes scattering in every which direction. Only three of the constructs actually made it to the destination bin. After the lively crowd quieted down, the emcee proceeded to read each of the three airmailed picks.

"First, we have Dan Robey, the turncoat who predicts Lincoln 37, Hamilton 3. Next is Lisa Bueller, who agrees with Dan on the winner but offers a closer score of 26 to 12." With the crowd hooting in derision, he read the last prediction. "My friends, we have a true Hamilton Bear in our midst. Tony Lucas predicts our guys will upset Lincoln by a score of 17 to 14."

The students let out an ear-splitting yell in appreciation of Tony's pick. In reality, his prediction seemed quite preposterous considering that Lincoln High dominated the rivalry and had won the last ten contests in a row, most by convincing margins.

The following Saturday, after the game had ended, the Lucases' quiet evening at home was shattered by an endless stream of phone calls. Each caller wanted to know how Tony foresaw the game's outcome, for indeed, the Bears had won by a score of 17 to 14. Rather than complain about their phone ringing off the hook, Tony's parents took in the entire episode with bemused expressions on their faces, content to appreciate their son's newfound popularity.

Another special characteristic that served Tony well in his academic studies was his dogged determination in researching and completing a task, no matter how difficult, to its successful conclusion. This was a trait he had inherited from his father, whose constant reminder to his children was a quote attributed to Albert Einstein: "It's not that I'm so smart; it's just that I stay with problems longer." Tony's parents had often praised him for his persistence in tackling and finishing difficult projects, noting that such a degree of tenaciousness was unusual in most children his age.

Perhaps because of this attribute, Tony was drawn to the subject of history, where assignments often required a persistent and dedicated research effort on some landmark event or some prominent figure. Although he had always enjoyed the subject in grammar school, he first developed a real passion for history as a high school freshman under the influence of his teacher, a kind man named Mr. Fleming, who literally brought the subject to life with his stirring lectures and fervent opinions. While Tony had originally considered following in his father's footsteps and pursuing a career in medicine, his fervor for history and his affinity for research projects convinced him that this subject was his true vocation.

Tony's fascination for history strengthened during his subsequent high school years as he participated in various school activities and clubs whose ethnic and topical diversity spanned from environmentalists to anti-war activists, each of whom demanded an outlet for their voices. In particular, the Vietnam War that was raging at the time energized a large, vocal contingent of student advocates lobbying for an end to that polarizing conflict. From his various interactions with such students, Tony began to appreciate that studying the past often provides a viable path to affect meaningful societal changes. Moreover, history was a topic consistent with Tony's obsession with time. After all, he thought. What is history but studying the past to try and prepare for the future?

By Tony's junior year, his accomplishments had completely validated his parent's choice that Hamilton High was the right school for him. "We are so proud of you," Tony's mother told him one evening after viewing another one of his report cards. "I love the comments from your teachers, especially the one from Mr. Gregory complimenting you on your history essay. You put so much effort into that project. I'm pleased he recognized that."

Dr. Lucas added, "And besides your great marks, you made first team cross country this year. You apply the same energy and determination to your running as you do to your studies. Those are really winning combinations."

Tony beamed with pride at his parent's comments. His comfort level at school would have been unimaginable just two years earlier. He had scored excellent grades, bonded with a small group of close friends, and developed into an accomplished member of the school's track team. His tall and slim physique, a result of a late teenage growth spurt, coupled with his natural persistence and tenacity, suited his penchant for distance running. During his races, he refused to succumb to the fatigue that often overpowered many of his teammates and competitors. Cross country, where trails stretched over a grueling three-mile course littered with potholes and steep uphill paths, was his specialty, and he developed into one of the better distance runners on the team. Running cross country races while proudly displaying the green and white colors of the Hamilton High Bears on his jersey were some of the proudest moments of his life.

CHAPTER SIX

Following his graduation from Hamilton High School, Tony enrolled at Colgate University, a leading liberal arts college with a prominent history department. Its beautiful, five-hundred-acre campus, surrounded by hills, lakes, and woods, was nestled in the rural setting of central New York State, approximately a four-hour drive from his home in Brooklyn. Colgate, with its sterling reputation and world-class professors, seemed like a propitious setting in which to continue his study of American history and to formulate career plans in that discipline. It turned out to be a wise decision.

The Colgate experience challenged Tony in different ways than high school. The idyllic campus and small-town vibe provided the perfect atmosphere for quiet contemplation and planning, especially after eighteen years in Brooklyn's urban cacophony. The university's myriad of clubs and organizations provided a rich network for self-discovery. Tony first learned of a non-partisan, national student organization, Democracy Matters, during his sophomore year. Energized by its mission to limit the influence of big money on the American political system, a principle that reflected the philosophy of the Founding Fathers, Tony worked tirelessly on behalf of the Colgate chapter. While organizing meetings, recruiting like-minded students, preparing and distributing informational material, and holding campus rallies, Tony developed previously untapped communication and leadership skills. These efforts also helped clarify his career goals. Imagining a future where he could influence students while pursuing his passion for American history, Tony decided that a college professorship was his calling.

Motivation drove Tony's success, and his scholastic accomplishments were rewarded by a fellowship to pursue doctoral studies at another university well-known for its history department, Rutgers University in New Brunswick, New Jersey. There he adopted a monk-like existence, focusing his efforts on the rigorous cycle of course work, qualifying examinations, and his doctoral dissertation. Reflecting a skepticism with many politicians of his day, his doctoral thesis titled "The Paradoxes of President Woodrow Wilson" explored the contrast between Wilson's public pacifist views and his somewhat underhanded and largely behind-the-scenes efforts to drive America into the First World War.

One late spring evening, an event that would forever shape the remainder of Tony's life and create an everlasting memory unfolded in his home-away-from-home, the student library. After downing a quick dinner of scrambled eggs and toast—Tony's culinary standards were such that any hot meal was considered a successful one—he drove his battered Ford from his studio apartment to the main Rutgers campus. A gray drizzle filled the air that evening, but Tony could make out a red horizon in the distance, a harbinger of better weather ahead, at least according to ancient mariners.

Entering the red brick library marked by a thick layer of ivy, Tony sought out his favorite spot, a small cubicle hidden from view behind a large stack of reference tomes. The overhead lights barely reached the small cubbyhole, casting a dim shadow over the entire work area. In his familiar surroundings and against the muted background noises of whispered murmurings and tapping pencils, Tony hit the switch for the desk lamp and settled in for another long night of research and writing.

Minutes into his intense studies, the shrill horn of the fire alarm shattered the peaceful environment. Bewildered, Tony joined the other patrons in congregating around the lobby's main desk area where a middle-aged woman, the librarian on duty, announced that everyone should calmly evacuate the premises until the source of the problem was located. Joining his colleagues in the mass exodus, Tony's attention suddenly shifted to a pretty, dark-haired girl who had sauntered next to him.

She turned toward Tony and said, "That's one way to break up the routine."

Caught off-guard by her remark, Tony mumbled in return, "Yeah, well, that alarm isn't doing me any favors with all the work I have to do." Inwardly he scolded himself as soon as the words left his mouth. Real smooth, he thought sarcastically. I'm sure my complaining will really impress her. Trying to recover, he asked, "What are you studying?"

"English literature. I'm finishing my masters."

"Good for you. That sounds so exciting."

Her warm smile and bemused expression calmed his tattered nerves as she replied, "Well, I've never heard anyone describe English lit as exciting. But I enjoy it and hope to teach it."

"I plan to teach as well. I'm finishing my doctoral studies in American history."

"Well, that does sound exciting."

Feeling more comfortable, Tony replied, "My name is Tony. Do you want to take a little walk while we wait for the library to reopen?"

"That sounds nice. I'm Ann."

Tony had read somewhere that first dates are unforgettable,

and after their casual stroll around the campus against the backdrop of a clearing, moonlit sky, he wholeheartedly agreed. Ann melted his heart with her combination of wit, charm, and graceful beauty. The conversation between them flowed as easily as if they had known each other their entire lives. Both had strong family roots, were children of physicians, loved animals, and were pursuing graduate degrees. She was even a Yankees fan! Ann, who hailed from Southern Delaware, or as she facetiously put it, "slower, lower Delaware," was completing her final semester of credits towards a master's degree.

By night's end, Tony felt such a connection with Ann that he confidently pronounced, "I think we are meant to be together."

In response, her face illuminated in a beaming smile, and she clasped her warm hand around his.

Tony's thesis and academic performance qualified him as an attractive candidate for many university positions, and upon graduation, he was offered an assistant professorship position at the University of Delaware, an expanding college located in Newark, Delaware, about thirty miles south of Philadelphia. Meanwhile, Ann started teaching English at a middle school in Lawrence Township, New Jersey, approximately an hour's drive north. Following a few years of interstate dating, Ann transferred to a parochial school in Wilmington, Delaware, aptly named St. Ann's, and shortly thereafter, they became engaged. Their wedding later that year was a small but festive event attended by family members and their few close friends. With their accumulated savings, they managed to make a down payment on a small house situated near the university where Tony worked and settled into a comfortable and harmonious routine.

The beautiful Delaware campus nestled on almost two thousand acres of pristine landscape suited Tony to a tee. Growing in confidence as he assumed increasing responsibilities in the history department, he progressed through the academic ranks and was viewed as "Chairman" material. His own history textbook, a laborious project of labor and love, cemented his reputation in the field. His real passion for history surfaced in the classroom, where he challenged students to apply lessons from the past to their current situations. By making history relevant for a younger generation, he became one of the more popular professors among the students.

Ann loved her job teaching English to seventh and eighth graders. She amazed Tony with her passion for education and with her ridiculous work schedule, often toiling late into the night reviewing and editing student essays. Tony firmly believed that English teachers were among the most underrated and underappreciated of professionals.

Outside of work, Tony and Ann's nurturing relationship blossomed over many shared activities and interests. Frigid winter months offered the opportunity to hit the slopes at local resorts. Tony had developed into a skillful skier from his time at Colgate; its proximity to several mountains had offered easy access to great downhill trails. Ann's innate athletic ability amazed Tony, and she quickly developed an aptitude and love for the sport.

Spring's warmer temperatures ushered in several outdoor pursuits that brought them closer together. Both loved tennis, and with their frequent matches, they developed into proficient players. Pounding the pavement of scenic trails that meandered through the rustic landscape of Delaware's state parks represented a welcome outlet for pent-up energy and stress. These runs reminded Tony of his cross-country days during his formative years in high school. *Unbelievable,* he often thought to himself. *I never thought I'd be so lucky to wind up with a running partner as perfect as Ann.*

The warmer weather also sparked a heightened level of excitement in their household with the dawn of a new baseball season. Watching their beloved Yankees on TV was another bonding experience, and venturing to the Bronx each summer to attend games at Yankee Stadium was an annual ritual.

During their first few years of marriage, they both fell under the spell of a mischievous tabby cat named Lester, who became the first in a line of feline companions.

Another enjoyable pastime for them was traveling, and their excursions included many trips to recreational destinations such as beaches and national parks. As a history scholar, Tony particularly relished the opportunity to explore landmark sites that provided a deeper engagement with archival events from the country's past.

Ann's ultimate dream vacation was to tour Spain, a country that had enthralled her ever since childhood. "We have to visit Spain," she would often tell Tony. "I think about it so much that I'm convinced it's going to be part of our destiny."

"Don't worry, dear. We'll get there someday."

Little did either of them know how correct her intuition would prove.

CHAPTER SEVEN

Tony's continued to display a freakish talent for predicting future events, even if most of the examples were trivial in nature. He often amazed Ann with his prognostications about topics as diverse as the correct arrival date for a particular delivery package or the precise time a plumber would appear to fix a leak in the kitchen faucet.

One afternoon she turned to him and said, "Tony, you may believe your obsession with time is useful for some mild entertainment, but did you ever think your gift could be used for something really important instead of just trivial predictions?"

Tony paused a second before responding, "I never thought much about that. Sometimes I just get a feeling about a future event that usually is no big deal. I hope it never gets more serious than that."

The following week, a chance encounter with a stranger would suggest to Tony that his fate may be intertwined with other individuals who shared a similar aptitude about time and, as a result, left him wondering about Ann's question.

As rabid Yankee fans, Tony and Ann enjoyed outings to Yankee Stadium in the Bronx, their normal venue for viewing ball games. One Saturday morning in early June of 1983, they noticed that the Yankees were on the road, scheduled to play the second of a three-game weekend series against the Baltimore Orioles at the Orioles' home field, Baltimore Memorial Stadium. Tony had a sudden idea.

"Ann, why don't we drive down to Baltimore for this afternoon's game? It's only an hour's drive down 95."

"That's a great idea. It's supposed to be a perfect afternoon, and I've never been to a game in Baltimore."

For them, few leisurely activities matched the excitement level of catching a live game with the Yankees, especially if their team came out on top. To their friends and family, most of whom had little emotional attachment to any professional sports team, it was difficult for Tony and Ann to describe the reverence with which they both held the Yankees. It was another example of their wonderful compatibility.

Later that morning, they piled into their silver car, a 1978 Ford Fairmont model that Tony had purchased at the start of his new position at the university, and drove to downtown Baltimore, the site of the stadium that was often referred to as "The Old Grey Lady of 33rd Street." After parking in one of the cheaper garages off Pratt Street, a good walking distance to the stadium, they strolled past throngs of boisterous fans almost equally divided in their team allegiances, as reflected by a fifty-fifty split in Yankees and Orioles paraphernalia, and eventually joined the rapidly growing ticket line.

At the box office, Tony purchased two lower-tier seats. It was then he noticed the signs indicating that the day game was a special promotional event. Most major league baseball teams had developed special promo days as a means of turning sparsely attended games into near or total sell-outs by providing free goodies for the fans. Today's freebie was an Orioles cap, available to the first thirty-thousand fans. Moreover, an additional bonus prize was available to a select group of attendees. Five ticket-buyers would have their seats randomly chosen and win free tickets to any single home game of their choice during the remainder of the season, another sixty or so games.

Tony gave little thought to baseball caps or future games as he and Ann settled into their seats to enjoy the afternoon baseball. It was a perfect, late-spring day, with the temperature hovering at 74° F and a gentle warm breeze blowing in from the right field. The game developed into a tight defensive struggle, marked by sterling pitching and outstanding defensive plays by both teams. Tony was totally immersed in the game, trying to predict managerial moves designed to engineer some runs for the visiting Yankees, when he heard the booming voice of the public address announcer over the stadium's loudspeakers.

"Fans, now is the time to take notice of your ticket stub, as I will be calling five seat numbers. Those seat holders will win two free tickets to any upcoming Orioles home game of their choice. If your seat is called, please report to Section Twenty under the grand concourse at the conclusion of the game to claim your prize."

In his distinct baritone voice, he proceeded to announce the winning seat numbers. After his fourth pronouncement, "Section 110, Row 8, Seat 5," Ann let out an excited yell, "Tony, that's your seat! You won!"

Tony's good fortune suddenly triggered memories of the last time he had won a prize in a drawing. It was in the eighth grade when Sister Constantia picked his name as the winner of the St. Bridget's time capsule contest. Taking the box home that day had proved to be the start of his strange experience with the key and the futuristic newspaper headlines. *I wonder if this win will turn out to be as mysterious,* he thought.

As the game continued, a late-inning rally by the Yankees secured a victory, adding the final feather to the cap of a delightful afternoon. When the final Orioles hitter went down on strikes, the fans began a mass evacuation of the stadium while Tony and Ann made their way down to the grand concourse to claim the prize. There were a few people already milling around the area; a teenage boy, a young woman with a small child, and a middle-aged man wearing a red T-shirt; these were probably the other winners. As the small group waited for a team official to appear, Tony began to examine the other winners in closer detail. Turning his attention to the man, Tony noticed the biggest watch he had ever seen strapped on the man's left wrist. The large dial reminded Tony of the type of watches aviators wore to read the time while they were flying. The wording on the front of the man's red T-shirt also made reference to time; it read, "Your time is our obsession." The back of the shirt listed the name and phone number of a store: Robert's Italian Emporium.

Tony kept his gaze directed at this man until Ann interrupted him with the words, "What are you staring at?"

There was just something about this individual and his outward displays of time references that made Tony wonder if meeting him here was something more than a chance encounter with a random stranger. Before Tony could answer Ann, a team official wearing a black Orioles cap appeared from behind the grandstand and started shouting in a loud voice. "Winners of the drawing. Please have your ticket stubs ready and form a line in front of me."

Only four of the five winners had appeared to claim their tickets, and Tony was the last in line. As his turn finally approached, the official asked. "May I see your ticket stub, please?"

Tony handed over the small stub as he replied, "Here it is. I guess it's my lucky day."

"Section 110, Row 8, Seat 5. That's the winning number. Congratulations! Now, what game would you like to see?"

Tony had already discussed possible dates with Ann as they reviewed the Orioles schedule in their program booklet, and they settled on September 15th, because he had another one of his premonitions that portended an important milestone for the Orioles at that particular game, even though their opponent was the Kansas City Royals and not his beloved Yankees. Ann would have preferred a future Yankees game, but she knew him too well to question his intuition about future events.

He answered. "September 15th against the Royals."

In response, the official gave him an inquisitive look before he spoke. "September 15th, that's a coincidence; there are over sixty games to choose from, and you and that fella with the red shirt over there both chose the same date. How strange is that? Are you in cahoots with him or something?"

"No, it's just a coincidence."

But was it just a coincidence? Choosing the same game only strengthened Tony's inkling that there was some kind of special connection between the two of them. Noticing the other winner standing in the corner drinking a soft drink, Tony approached him, extended his right arm, and spoke. "Hi, my name is Tony. I understand we both picked the September 15th game. I was curious why you chose that date."

The man looked up at Tony—he was several inches shorter and much stockier in build. Taking Tony's right hand in a firm grasp that conveyed both strength and warmth, he answered, "Hi, I'm Robert. So, you picked the fifteenth too? That's interesting. I'm a huge Orioles fan, and I just have a feeling that the fifteenth is going to be a big day for the team. Just between us, I'm usually pretty good at predicting these things. Some of my friends think I'm a bit nuts, but I'm usually right when it comes to dates and time." Eyeing Tony's Yankees jersey, Robert continued, "I think the more interesting question is, why did a Yankees fan pick that date? The Orioles are playing Kansas City that day."

Tony was stunned. This man apparently shared a similar intuition with Tony, and he had used that instinct to choose the

September 15th game, just as Tony had. He replied in a wavering tone, "I just believe the fifteenth will be an important date for your Orioles, and I want to be here to see it."

"Wow, sounds like we might have something in common. I'd love to talk more about baseball and predictions with you, but I better get going now. My wife is home with our baby daughter, Rosa, and if I don't get back soon, she'll never let me go to another game. Nice meeting you, Tony."

As the stranger disappeared, Tony wondered if meeting Robert was some kind of signal that their fates were intertwined. He dismissed this thought as too far-fetched. It would be another thirty-six years before Tony would discover the real answer to his question.

CHAPTER EIGHT

Tony remembered the summer of 1983 for a number of reasons. One was the relentless heat that pressed over much of the continental United States, literally every day and late into the evening hours. In Wilmington, July and August were characterized by several stifling days, with temperatures reaching the high nineties. Tony often observed the late afternoon heat bouncing off the streets and causing an illusion of shimmering images. It reminded him of his father's words years ago when Tony accompanied him during a house call on one brutally hot summer day in Brooklyn. "These sidewalks are hot enough to fry an egg." Tony was sure that was the case now; the summer heat was almost unbearable.

It was also in 1983 that he first heard the term "global warming." Rumblings from environmentalists suggested that the smothering temperatures resulted from man-made carbon emissions trapping heat radiating from earth towards space. Left unchecked, the experts postulated that this so-called "greenhouse effect" posed an existential threat to future generations. Tony wondered if industrialized countries were willing to acknowledge this problem and take remedial actions before it was too late. Unfortunately, his study of history had taught him that many problems affecting civilizations were allowed to develop into crises before they were taken seriously.

For relief from the withering heat, Tony and Ann made frequent day trips to Rehoboth in southern Delaware, near where Ann had been raised, to enjoy the refreshing waters of the Atlantic and the cooling sea breezes. Visits to the ocean had been an important part of their childhoods that they now enjoyed together.

As summer drew to a close and the September 15th game date arrived, Tony's thoughts turned to the unmemorable Yankees season. After a strong start, they sputtered to a non-contending position with only ten games remaining. Ironically, the highlight of the season had been one of the craziest games in Yankees history, the infamous Pine Tar Game. Playing Kansas City in late July at Yankee Stadium, Royals star George Brett hit a ninth-inning home run to give his team the lead. However, Yankees manager Billy Martin, no stranger to histrionics, asked the umpires to examine Brett's bat for excessive pine tar. After a series of lengthy discussions and measurements, they ruled that the amount of pine tar on the bat's handle exceeded the allotted quantity and ruled Brett out. The Royals' reaction, particularly that of Brett, who stormed out of the dugout to stalk the home plate umpire like a raging maniac, became one of the most unforgettable scenes in baseball history. After the game, won by the Yankees, the Royals protested the result with the American League, who upheld their claim, and the game was resumed weeks later with Brett's home run now allowed. This time the Royals went on to win the contest, and a legendary game in Yankees lore was established, although not with the result that Yankees fans desired.

In contrast, the Orioles rode a spectacular second-half record to a commanding lead in the division and tonight were poised to claim the Eastern Division crown with a win. As Ann and he drove down the interstate to the old Baltimore ballpark for the night game, she said, "Well, it looks as if you were right again about the importance of this game. It could be the clincher for the Orioles."

"We'll see," replied Tony. "I wonder if Robert, the other guy who had the same feeling about the game as me, will show up. I'd like to talk to him some more about this time thing we both seem to have."

"Great," replied Ann in a joking tone. "That's all I need, surrounded by a group of time savants."

Jockeying through the excited throngs of fans anxious to celebrate the pinnacle of a successful regular season, Tony and Ann approached their seats located in a lower-tier box on the third-base side of the field. Tony immediately began to scan the area for Robert; however, he was nowhere to be seen. Perhaps he couldn't get away for the game; after all, he did have that young baby daughter, Rosa.

The game progressed uneventfully, at least in terms of any extracurricular activities, and the Orioles fulfilled Tony and Robert's predictions by clinching the American East Division with a sharply played 5-2 victory. The outcome only strengthened Tony's conviction that both of their fates were somehow inextricably linked, and he regretted Robert's absence and the opportunity to discuss their mutual abilities.

CHAPTER NINE

The year ended with exhilarating news for Ann and Tony, for they learned she was pregnant with their first child. Anxious to start a family, they were thrilled at the prospect of a new baby. Equally delighted were both sets of parents; this would be the first grandchild in both families. When their precious baby arrived several months later, a beautiful little girl they christened Monica, she was naturally smothered with the love and attention befitting a firstborn. Ann and Tony settled into parental mode quite naturally, readily adjusting their lifestyles to conform to the needs of an infant. Three years later, a period that seemed like a non-stop adventure for Ann and Tony, a baby boy they named Andrew joined their family.

The children provided endless joy to both parents, and neither Ann nor Tony could imagine their lives without kids. It was especially enjoyable for the parents to observe the genesis of their children's individual personalities and characteristics. Although both children were even-tempered and sweet in disposition, Monica, as the elder sibling, developed a somewhat dominant nature, especially when interacting with her baby brother. Andrew soon reached a stage in his development where he exerted his own independence, and Monica's constant admonitions often grated on him, resulting in frequent squawks and tantrums. More and more often, Ann and Tony found themselves assuming roles as mediators over vital disputes such as toy ownership, bath times, and first dibs on desserts and other treats. It reminded Tony of his childhood years growing up in a household with loving parents and his older, somewhat domineering sister Karen. Ann and Tony viewed sibling squabbles as a natural part of child-rearing and did their best to discourage such behavior without overly worrying about their children's spats. After all, Tony remained close to Karen, hosting her frequent visits in Delaware or traveling to her home in Jacksonville, Florida, on a regular basis. Karen, who worked as a bank executive, and Ann had also developed a warm friendship and treated each other as sisters.

One muggy August evening in 1988, the Lucases were assembled in their family room, the central gathering place for the family. As usual, the floor was littered with children's toys, blocks, and miscellaneous playthings; no matter how much effort Ann and Tony dedicated to keeping a neat household, they could never seem to keep up with their young children's abilities to wreak havoc on any environment they inhabited. Four-year-old Monica was role-playing the part of a dictatorial teacher, so consistent with her assertive personality, instructing her two-year-old brother in counting lessons. Ann was sitting in the corner of the room, reading the newspaper and checking on the weather forecast for the upcoming weekend. Tony lounged in front of the TV, casually viewing the opening night ceremonies of the 1988 Democratic convention in Atlanta, where the delegates had gathered to nominate their presidential candidate. Noticing the children playing so nicely together, Tony laughed to himself and thought, *How did a shy, introverted kid from Brooklyn wind up with a loving wife and children, living in a two-story colonial home nestled in one of the suburban, tree-lined neighborhood communities of North Wilmington, Delaware?* He happily reminisced about the circuitous journey that had led him here from his Brooklyn roots and his wonderful fortune meeting Ann during those final days of graduate school.

Tony's thoughts returned to the present as he heard Ann asking him questions about possible weekend plans. "It's supposed to be nice this Saturday. Why don't we run down to the beach for the day? The kids would love playing in the sand and the water and visiting Funland." The latter was a beloved local amusement park nestled on the Rehoboth Beach boardwalk and packed with rides and attractions for families and small children. "We could stop and visit my parents on the way home." Ann's parents retained the house where Ann had grown up, located in Sussex County at the lower end of Delaware, approximately a twenty-minute drive from the beach.

"Sounds good to me," answered Tony. He was always up for a seaside outing with the family.

As Ann continued her musings on possible weekend plans, Tony suddenly returned his attention to the TV screen displaying the Democratic convention, where Governor Michael Dukakis of Massachusetts was the predestined presidential candidate for the party. But it was another name that had caught Tony's ear. He hopped out of his chair and quickly moved towards the TV to raise the volume. As he did so, he yelled, "Quiet," in such a stern voice that Ann and the children were startled into sudden silence. Tony listened attentively as the TV reporter continued his discourse.

"Now, to present the official nomination speech for Governor Dukakis is a rising star in the Democratic Party, Governor Bill Clinton of Arkansas."

Tony was dumbfounded. Rarely had he thought about that strange day in the eighth grade so many years ago; mostly, he had laid those newspaper headlines of the future to rest. But the name Bill Clinton had triggered an instant reaction; that was the name of the supposed president whose special appointment as an envoy was proclaimed in the front-page story of the 2025 newspaper. Except for that one story all those years ago, Tony had never heard of Bill Clinton. Yet here he was on the TV screen, the governor of Arkansas, with probable aspirations to be a future presidential candidate. Tony knew the high-profile nominating speech was generally assigned to an individual the party viewed as future presidential material. It was all too much to be a coincidence.

"What's wrong?" asked Ann, jarring Tony out of his trance.

"Nothing, dear. I have to go look for something."

He turned away and sprinted upstairs to his bedroom. Stashed on the very back of his closet shelf was the battered toy safe from his old Brooklyn home. It was one of the few items from his childhood that he still kept as an adult. He removed the safe and turned the simple two-wheel combination lock, left to nineteen and right to five, to open it. Removing the old, crumpled piece of paper, he reviewed his notes from that late summer day in 1965.

There it was in his own scribble; former President Bill Clinton appointed as envoy to Sudan. Tony now realized that two of the three stories from that newspaper were at least partially validated. The 1965 Yankees had indeed collapsed, finishing that season in sixth place and initiating a decade-long era of frustration. And while Bill Clinton wasn't yet president, he seemed poised to claim that crown sometime in the future. Tony turned his attention to his notes on the final story, a miracle cure for a crippling disease. He thought, *I wonder if I could somehow use this information to advance a cure for some dreadful illness.* However, the information from the story was so limited and vague, with no specifics on the cure, its inventor, or even the disease itself, that Tony abandoned this idea. Nevertheless, as he placed the sheet of paper back in the safe, he had a strange feeling that this information, as meager as it was, would someday prove invaluable to him.

CHAPTER TEN

September 1, 2018

"Are you all right?" cried Tony as his serve skirted the back line of Ann's service box.

"I think so," answered Ann as she lay sprawled on the ground. "I must have just tripped."

Hopping over the net in one smooth motion and running to her side, Tony said, "Let me help you up."

"I think I need a minute to recover."

"Take as long as you need."

As Tony waited with Ann, he started to wonder about their recent tennis outings. Over the years, their matches had been highly competitive, with Tony emphasizing consistent and powerful groundstrokes in his game, while Ann matched him with superb net play and a wicked spin serve. However, in recent weeks Ann's play had deteriorated to such a level that most games wound up lopsided in Tony's favor. At first, he had given it little thought. But now, with Ann's game eroding at an alarming rate, other physical manifestations of weakness were appearing as well. Frequently the racquet would slide out of her grip after hitting a shot, and falling on the court had become a regular occurrence. Pensively he thought, *What is going on with*

Ann? Is there something that could put a dent in our carefully thought-out plans?

Tony was a very robust sixty-seven and in excellent health. Ann was one year younger, and until recently, had been more than a match for him in most of the physical activities in which they engaged. Not wanting to neglect family, personal interests, and favorite pastimes at the expense of too much time and energy at work, they both had recently retired from successful and fulfilling careers.

Tony's long span as a professor at the university had culminated in his appointment as Chairman of the History Department, just as had been foreshadowed several years before. In this role, he had spent years revamping the curriculum, molding it in the image he envisioned for a leading learning center of American studies, and transforming it into one of the university's more progressive departments. Specifically, this entailed an increased emphasis on Black history, a subject often ignored or trivialized because it illuminated America at its worst. Tony recognized that Black history laid the foundation for many of the monumental events in the nation's past and was, therefore, an essential component of any comprehensive curriculum.

His other major initiative had been to expand the university's graduate program and its funding, appreciating the advantages that his doctoral program at Rutgers University all those years ago had afforded him.

After a successful tenure, during which time his name became synonymous with American history throughout the Delaware campus, the urge to spend more time with Ann and the rest of his family, including his four grandchildren, prompted him to retire. Now, as Chairman Emeritus, he still maintained a level of involvement in the profession he loved, teaching an undergraduate course in American history at the university.

Ann had also enjoyed a rewarding teaching career and,

just within the last year, had been persuaded to join Tony in retirement. Neither of them would ever forget the moving celebration when, in honor of her years of dedicated service to St. Ann's, school officials had dedicated the new library in her name. As with Tony, she still maintained an occasional teaching presence, periodically substituting for former colleagues when they called in sick. It was just enough of a commitment to keep her satisfied but not overwhelmed.

They believed that life held many more experiences in store for them, and retiring at this stage afforded them the opportunity to enjoy many active and rewarding years together. Aside from family affairs, their pursuits included tennis, jogging, hiking, writing, and traveling. Tony had already promised their first overseas trip would be an extensive tour of Spain, Ann's dream vacation destination since childhood. They also planned to visit as many of America's beautiful national parks as possible. Last year's trip to Yellowstone National Park with its awe-inspiring vistas and fascinating geothermal wonders had reinvigorated the sense of adventure in both of them.

Fortunately, Tony and Ann were in a financial position to support the type of retirement lifestyle they envisioned. Although they lived in a relatively frugal manner, they had accumulated sufficient savings, pensions, and social security benefits over the years so that their economic situation was quite adequate for meeting their needs. Tony quietly breathed a prayer of thanks for Chesley Pritchard, the young financial advisor whom they had consulted with years ago, shortly after their marriage. He had persuaded them way back in 1982 to make regular contributions to an S&P 500 mutual fund, well before such index investments became fashionable. Talk about good timing! Over the years, their nest egg had ballooned into a substantial portfolio that contributed greatly to their financial security and comfortable lifestyle.

They owned a classic two-story colonial in suburban North Wilmington and had raised their two children there. Funding college and graduate degree programs for both kids had spared Monica and Andrew the debt burden that was ravaging so many of their friends. Tony and Ann were extremely proud of their children; in addition to having great families, both kids had achieved academic and professional success. Monica was an interior designer for a leading commercial firm based in Philadelphia, while Andrew worked as an IT specialist for one of Wilmington's large financial firms. Ann and Tony enjoyed nothing more than spending time with their family; how great it was that both children lived nearby.

These days, aside from charitable donations, annual family vacations at the beach, periodic trips, and the never-ending costs of home ownership and repair, their major financial outlays seemed aimed at totally spoiling their grandkids. Retirement provided them the opportunity to become a regular part of their four grandchildren's lives; there just weren't enough words in the dictionary to describe how Tony and Ann felt about them. A quote attributed to the comedy writer Gene Perret probably summed up their feelings best. "What a bargain grandchildren are! I give them my loose change, and they give me a million dollars worth of pleasure."

They also maintained their roles as pet parents, having adopted a black and white kitten named Holly a few years ago, their fourth cat in a continuous line of pet ownership since their first cat Lester. Holly developed a particular affinity for Ann, often pulling out all stops for her attention, such as meowing out loud, knocking objects off the table, or pawing at her passing legs until Ann consented to pick her up and stroke her back.

Shaking Tony out of his musings, Ann asked. "Could you help me up? I feel better now."

"Of course, honey; here, take my hand. Let's call it a day."

"Oh, no," replied Ann. "It's so nice out; let's go one more set."

All in all, thought Tony, *our life together has been a great ride. And the best is yet to come. At least, I hope it is!*

CHAPTER ELEVEN

The crystal chandelier emitted a lustrous beam of light that reflected the bright colors from the floral centerpiece, adding to the festive atmosphere. Elegantly dressed in their finest linen tablecloth and ornamented with the Lucases' best china, the rectangular dining room table had become the focal point for Tony and Ann's thirty-eighth wedding anniversary celebration.

Where have all the years gone? wondered Tony. It seemed like just yesterday Ann and he were changing diapers, visiting grandparents, and romping through the yard with their young children. Now here they were, grandparents themselves, celebrating their beautiful marriage.

"What are you thinking about. Dad?" asked his daughter Monica. "You look as if you are in a trance."

Tony smiled and answered, "Just how lucky I am to have your mother as my wife."

Today, the entire family had assembled at their home to celebrate the festive event. The clan included Monica, her husband Jim, and their two children, seven-year-old Paul and four-year-old Katie, along with Andrew, his wife Mary, five-year-old William, and one-year-old Emma. A sudden pang of regret flooded through Tony's veins as he rued the absence of his parents. Ironically, they had succumbed to the ravages of old age within twelve months of each other, approximately ten years ago. Tony recalled with affection how his parents had supported him through those difficult, early days at high school all those years ago. He thought, My mom's advice when I was a freshman literally turned my life around. Their indelible footprints had shaped not only Tony's and Ann's lives but had also created a lasting legacy of love and support for Monica and Andrew as they grew into young adults. Tony only hoped to have a similar impact on the lives of his own grandchildren.

A sudden deafening sound shattered Tony out of his serene reflections. Looking up, he noted Ann's exasperated expression and heard her plaintive sobbing.

"Oh no! what have I done?"

"It's okay, Mother," answered Monica. "It's only a dessert."

"It's more than that!" she cried out. "It's a German chocolate anniversary cake that I specially ordered at Luchow's. And now, it's completely ruined." Distraught, she ran from the dining room into the kitchen.

As the family recovered from the unsettling incident, Monica turned to her father and asked. "What's wrong with Mother? She seems so edgy lately, and that cake isn't the only thing she dropped this evening."

"I'm sure it's nothing," answered Tony more confidently than he felt. "This anniversary has probably put your mother in a reflective mood. She'll be fine. If you and Andrew can help clean up this mess, I'll go talk with her."

As he strode out of the dining room to comfort his wife, Tony couldn't shake the sense of gloom emanating from the back of his mind. These troublesome incidents were occurring more frequently, and Tony wasn't the only one to notice.

It was probably only arthritis settling into her joints, he reminded himself. Tony recalled reading that everyone over a certain age was bound to develop some degree of arthritis. Our joints were just not designed to last the typical lifespan of modern humans. Indeed, their family physician, Dr. Smith, suggested that was probably the cause of her problems, especially since both of Ann's parents had suffered from osteoarthritis. But following that appointment a few weeks ago, Ann's symptoms had worsened to include occasions of slurred speech, periodic tripping episodes, and unusual emotional outbursts, such as that which the family had just witnessed.

That's when Dr. Smith recommended a consultation with a neurologist, Dr. Henry Gladstone.

Tony found Ann sitting on the island stool in the kitchen. "Well," he said, trying to lighten the mood. "You really know how to make an entrance."

"What's wrong with me, Tony?" pleaded Ann. "I seem to be falling apart."

"It's okay. Remember what Dr. Smith said. Arthritis runs in your family. And just to be sure, we will visit Dr. Gladstone on Tuesday. Now let's get back to the celebration. The grandkids are wondering where Nana disappeared to."

"Well, it's lucky I didn't ruin the ice cream along with the cake. At least we can have some dessert."

Ann gave Tony a warm hug, and, comforted by his calming support, she made her way back to the family gathering.

CHAPTER TWELVE

With a high degree of trepidation, Tony and Ann drove up the street, housing an office complex that was populated with a series of cookie-cutter, two-story, red-brick buildings. Following the signs for Neurology Practice of Delaware, Tony parked the car, and they ambled past a myriad of pedestrians along a stone-paved pathway leading to a large, sliding glass door entrance. Proceeding down a maze of corridors, they entered Dr. Gladstone's waiting room for Ann's 2 p.m. appointment.

The reception area was small but tidy and contained only six empty chairs with a pair of matching oval coffee tables on either end. Piled in neat rows on each table were a cluster of beautifully illustrated coffee-table books on topics as diverse as gardening, travel, and wild animals. In the back, a large rectangular fish tank filled with colorful and exotic fish emitted a rhythmic, gurgling sound. The entire area radiated an aura of relaxation and calm.

Ann announced her arrival to the receptionist positioned behind a glass enclosure and completed the necessary paperwork. In short order, a tall man with erect posture, whose professional dress complete with a white coat and clearly marked nametag inspired confidence, stepped out to greet them. He appeared about ten years or so younger than Tony.

In a pleasant tone, he spoke out, "Good afternoon. I'm

Henry Gladstone."

"I'm Ann Lucas, and this is my husband Anthony," replied Ann.

Shaking both of their hands, he replied, "It's nice to meet both of you. Now please follow me back to the examining room. Mr. Lucas, feel free to join us."

Entering the small room, Dr. Gladstone gestured for Ann and Tony to take the two available chairs and, motioning to a small, middle-aged lady standing in the back, said, "This is Sarah, my nurse. Now, what brings you here today?"

Ann quickly described her symptoms as Tony sat listening. Periodically, Dr. Gladstone would interrupt with a probing question to gather additional information.

"Well, let's have a look," responded Dr. Gladstone.

Following a quick physical and neurological examination, Dr. Gladstone pronounced, "Nothing is obvious, although you do show signs of reduced sensation and reflex response in your arms and legs. I'd like to schedule you for some diagnostic tests. The results will help us rule out several possibilities and get us much closer to the root of the problem."

Ann asked the very question Tony was thinking. "What are some of the possible causes?"

"Well," responded Dr. Gladstone. "It's really too early to speculate, but your symptoms could be due to any of a number of diseases, not all of which are neurological. These include thyroid disease, hepatitis, or some autoimmune disease. Vitamin B12 deficiency could also explain your problems; I noticed you don't take a B12 supplement."

Dr. Gladstone spent a few more minutes answering some general questions and then finished with these parting words. "Sarah will set up the tests, which should take a couple of weeks. I'll call you after I review the results, and we can then schedule a follow-up appointment."

Ann and Tony emerged from the office with a sense of cautious optimism. Dr. Gladstone's calm demeanor and his rational plan for a series of clinical tests had instilled a degree of confidence that was lacking just hours ago. Nevertheless, neither of them could escape the cloud of worry that lurked in the back of their minds.

Over the next few weeks, Ann was subjected to a battery of scans and procedures, including blood and urine analysis, X-rays, MRIs, and a spinal tap. The lab tests also included a nerve conduction velocity study and an electromyography designed to determine how her muscles and nerves were acting. With the completion of these last tests, Ann and Tony bided their time as they anxiously awaited a call from Dr. Gladstone.

CHAPTER THIRTEEN

Tony leaned back in his leather-upholstered easy chair in their family room, ignoring the plaintive cries of Holly the cat meowing for attention. The somber words from Dr. Gladstone still reverberated through his head.

"Mrs. and Mr. Lucas. I'm afraid the news is not good. The composite results of your neurological tests indicate you have amyotrophic lateral sclerosis, commonly referred to as ALS."

ALS was a particularly insidious disease that progressively eroded a patient's physical capacities and mental facilities. Tony thought, *What a cruel way to initiate the next phase of our lives!* It still didn't seem real to him, and he couldn't begin to imagine the consequences.

As Tony would have predicted, Ann accepted her fate with a calm demeanor and no outward displays of emotion or complaints; no sobbing of, "Why me?" or, "It's not fair." But Tony could tell the bleak diagnosis had crushed her spirit, her very soul. And how could it not? All their well-laid plans for enjoying their retirement years were essentially shattered by a few short sentences from Dr. Gladstone. Even their daily ritual of completing the local newspaper's daily crossword puzzle would be compromised. Tony had always marveled at Ann's ability to solve challenging puzzle clues for which he had no idea. He shuddered in anxiety as he tried to imagine life without her.

Tony was out of his league with most medical issues and, in fact, knew very little about ALS except that it was a disease of the nervous system that caused increased paralysis over time. As he recalled, most patients didn't live for many years after an initial diagnosis. He also knew it was commonly referred to as Lou Gehrig's disease after the famed Yankee slugger who died of its complications. Tony recalled the old movie Pride of the Yankees that he had watched countless times as a kid. How ironic, thought Tony. Ann's diagnosis reminds us of one of the saddest moments in the history of our favorite team. He also recollected another famous victim of the disease, theoretical physicist Stephen Hawking, who spent his adult life anchored to a wheelchair while studying the mysteries of black holes. He thought, *Didn't Hawking have some special type of the disease that allowed him to live for years after his initial diagnosis?* Upset at his own ignorance about the disease and its potential treatments, he slammed his fist hard against the arm of his chair in frustration. Silently, he vowed to research every aspect of ALS and leave no stone unturned in an effort to help Ann through this ordeal. *If there is an effective treatment or, by some miracle, a cure out there, somewhere,* he thought, *I will find it!*

The first step in this quest for knowledge was their follow-up visit with Dr. Gladstone. The following day, Tony drove Ann to the office for her appointment. The empty waiting room seemed darker and gloomier than Tony remembered from their last visit. Even the brightly colored fish in the large aquarium stayed out of sight, hiding among the rocks and driftwood that littered the floor of the tank.

Dr. Gladstone greeted them with an empathetic expression and said, "Come on back."

Ann and Tony followed him into his small office and took the two proffered seats facing his large oak desk. Volumes of thick medical and neurology textbooks lined the shelves of his bookcase, and an array of diplomas and awards decorated the walls. Tony thought, somewhat sarcastically, *All these accolades mean little if Dr. Gladstone can't save Ann from this ordeal.*

"So, how are you feeling?" Dr. Gladstone asked Ann.

"As well as could be expected," Tony thought he heard her reply, for, in reality, he was in a trance-like state still trying to cope with the terrible news. *Shape up,* he thought to himself. *Imagine what poor Ann is going through. I have to be strong and alert for her.*

"I'm sure you have hundreds of questions," continued Dr. Gladstone, "so let's begin. I want to describe the basic pathology of ALS, its probable causes, and, most importantly, the treatment options for Ann. Please interrupt me along the way with any questions you may have. Hopefully, I will cover most of your concerns."

Tony and Ann nodded in assent, and Dr. Gladstone began. "ALS is actually a grouping of neurological diseases that progresses as motor neurons, the nerve cells in the brain that are responsible for relaying messages via electrical impulses to the spinal cord and muscles, die over time. As would be expected, the degeneration of neurons causes muscles to stop functioning, leading to their atrophy and the resulting paralysis."

Tony recalled the old adage for muscle tissue he had heard in the past, "Use it or lose it." He asked, "Is there any way to induce the muscle or nerve cells to grow back?"

Dr. Gladstone responded, "That's a great question. While there are exciting new discoveries in the area of cell regeneration, that is the growth of new cells to replace lost or damaged ones, we are still only at the early research stage in terms of promoting new muscle or nerve cell growth in vivo or in a living organism."

Expressing concern about her family, Ann asked, "Is there a risk that either of my children could develop ALS?"

Dr. Gladstone replied, "ALS is broadly classified into two types; sporadic is by far the most common type in the United States, representing up to ninety-five percent of all cases, while the familial type has a genetic component due to its occurrence in a particular family lineage. Scientists have identified more than forty genes, those are the small sections of DNA that represent the functional units of inheritance that may cause or contribute to familial ALS. However, since you have no known history of ALS in your family, I'm confident yours is sporadic in nature, and the risk to your children is minimal."

Dr. Gladstone's confident tone and extensive knowledge reminded Tony of a teacher lecturing his students. If only the subject were history or English, and not a life and death struggle with an insidious disease!

Next, he turned to a discussion of probable causes of sporadic ALS. "In most cases, the precise cause of ALS is unknown. A number of potential contributing factors have been identified, including exposure to environmental toxins and dysfunction of mitochondria, which are small intracellular organelles responsible for generating the energy molecules all cells require. Other possible causes include abnormalities in the body's immune system, chemical imbalances, particularly in specific chemical neurotransmitters that conduct nerve impulses to muscles and other nerve cells, and oxidative stress, which is an imbalance in the ratio of beneficial antioxidant molecules and dangerous free radical molecules. Different forms of the disease may have different causes."

Tony asked, "With so many possible causes, are there any treatments for ALS that work?"

"That question is a perfect lead-in for the next topic," Dr. Gladstone replied. "Unfortunately, no cure exists for ALS, and in spite of exciting research developments, none is likely to appear in the foreseeable future. However, two ALS treatment drugs have actually been approved by the FDA, the government's federal agency that authorizes all new drugs. An older drug, riluzole, acts by blocking glutamate, an important neurotransmitter chemical whose excess levels lead to the deterioration of nerve cells. A newer drug called edaravone apparently works by relieving the effects of oxidative stress. Unfortunately, both drugs have only modest effects on slowing disease progression in certain subsets of ALS patients. Neither drug can be classified as anything close to a cure. A true wonder drug or golden bullet, as such a miracle cure is referred to in the pharmaceutical industry, would be an agent that promoted the regeneration of neurons. As I already mentioned, neurons lack the capacity to divide and replicate. Therefore, once specific nerve cells are destroyed, the important functions those cells perform in transmitting electrical impulses to muscles are lost."

In a voice trembling with dread, Ann asked the question that weighed most on their minds. "Dr. Gladstone, how much longer do I have?"

"That's a very difficult question, both to ask and to answer. The disease progression can vary widely. Most patients with ALS will live for three to five years after experiencing symptoms, but around ten percent may live for ten years or longer. At this point, I can't provide any more details than those general statistics."

Tony squirmed uncomfortably in his seat and grabbed the handrails of his chair with his clammy palms. Looking over at Ann, he noticed her ashen face frozen in an expression of resigned acceptance. Dr. Gladstone's words were not what they were hoping to hear. As if being on the receiving end of an ALS diagnosis wasn't grim enough, the uncertainty about Ann's future added to their despair.

"So what do I do now?" asked Ann.

Dr. Gladstone responded, "I'd like you to start on riluzole immediately. I'll write you a prescription today. Fortunately, there is a generic version, so the price is not prohibitive. I want to see you back here every few weeks to track your symptoms so we can develop a clearer picture of the disease progression. In the meantime, I would urge you to join some of the patient advocacy groups for ALS, such as the ALS Association. These organizations help patients and their families cope with the struggles of living with the disease by providing a wealth of resources on all aspects of ALS. Sarah will provide you with some brochures on your way out. Finally, I can't stress enough the importance of keeping your spirits up and maintaining a healthy attitude. I know this disease is terrifying, but you have to go on, and positive outlooks can make a huge difference in both of your lives."

With those parting words, he escorted them back to the waiting room and bid them farewell.

CHAPTER FOURTEEN

The drive home was oddly silent as Ann and Tony each tried to process the sobering words from Dr. Gladstone. With his head pounding from the mental exertion, Tony barely managed to avoid swerving into one of the many freestanding mailboxes that dotted the roadside. Dr. Gladstone had barely scratched the surface on the science of ALS, and yet these snippets of information had virtually overwhelmed his mental capacity. How could he, a mere history teacher, possibly succeed in finding a cure for a disease when brilliant scientists across the globe had been unsuccessful? Was he kidding himself? Turning toward Ann, her sorrowful expression suddenly boosted his resolve. Remember, he thought, leave no stone unturned. He may not have been a scientist of world renown, but as an accomplished historian, he was accustomed to exhaustive research campaigns in the pursuit of scholarly endeavors. Since boyhood, his persistence in completing such difficult tasks had always been one of his strengths. Now he would have to bring all his skills and tenacity to bear on this daunting problem. The stakes here were so much more profound than any other challenge he had ever faced; they were literally life and death.

Over the next several days, Tony completely immersed himself in his arduous quest at the expense of virtually all other activities. Nearly every waking moment not devoted to caring for Ann, whose physical capabilities were deteriorating at an alarming rate, was spent reading and studying scientific articles from various web sources, exploring detailed information provided on ALS patient advocacy sites, and collating data sources from the University of Delaware's huge library. As a retired professor, he retained his access to this vital resource with its treasure trove of medical journals and texts. Fortunately, Tony's adult children, Monica and Andrew, spent as much time as their busy schedules permitted in assisting their mother, freeing Tony from many mundane household tasks.

The family had also started to spread the word about Ann's condition to close friends and relatives and, as a result, were inundated with callers and visitors inquiring about her health. This included a brief visit from Tony's sister, Karen, who worked as a manager at Morgan Stanley in Florida and was very close to Ann. Tony fondly recalled Karen's response during the phone call when he informed her about Ann's illness.

"I'll be there tomorrow."

She dropped everything to fly north, thought Tony, taking some comfort in the unconditional support from his family.

Tony was also moved by the outpouring of kindness from so many people, although it did sometimes hamper his research efforts. There was just so much information to review, and often he felt overwhelmed, especially as he regularly neglected one of the important points that Dr. Gladstone had emphasized.

"While the toll of the disease on Ann is obvious, don't forget the burden it takes on immediate family members," cautioned Dr. Gladstone. "Make sure to take care of yourself as well as your wife. You will need your strength and your health to endure this crisis."

Indeed, Tony had virtually forsaken all his usual habits and activities to focus on his work. How could he fail to devote every waking moment to his wife and soul mate who meant the world to him? He could never forgive himself for doing anything less.

CHAPTER FIFTEEN

Huddled in front of his iMac for another late night of research, Tony yawned loudly as he peered at the incomprehensible title of the research paper glaring from his screen, "Amyotrophic lateral sclerosis-like symptoms in a patient with prosopagnosia experiencing disruption in postganglionic synapses associated with projection tracts." He thought, *How am I supposed to understand this stuff? I feel like that old dog that you can't teach new tricks. Cantonese would be easier to learn.*

Tony hit the Command-P keys on his keyboard to print the displayed article. Retrieving the pages and puncturing the edges with a three-hole punch, he added them to a growing stack in a three-ring binder emblazoned with the words University of Delaware History Department. Colored tabs separated the binder contents into three sections: ALS Background, Therapies, and Future Developments. Closing the binder, he noticed that section on therapies was by far the thinnest. Par for the course, he thought. The more desperately you want something, the less likely you are to get it.

In spite of his growing frustrations, Tony had managed to uncover a few exploratory themes over the past several days that at least provided a foundation for his future research efforts. First was a deeper appreciation for the true complexity of the brain. Scientists estimated that there are up to eighty-six billion neurons or nerve cells in the brain itself. On average, each neuron is connected to one thousand other neurons via functional junctions called synapses. This creates a tremendously complex network of communication composed of about a thousand trillion synapses, a number greater than the number of stars in the Milky Way galaxy. Tony could hardly comprehend such numbers. No wonder why many neuroscientists referred to the brain as the most complex object in the known universe. This incredible complexity was a major deterrent in understanding brain disease pathologies and, therefore, in developing effective treatments.

Another theme Tony uncovered was that while many innovative research technologies were being investigated for the potential treatment of severe neurological diseases such as ALS, they all shared one common descriptor—futuristic. The section of his binder on Future Developments was filled with papers ending with phrases such as, "may one day represent a novel approach for developing a new class of therapies for ALS." *Why isn't anything available now when we need it?* he thought.

If Ann's situation wasn't so dire, he certainly would have developed a greater appreciation for the amazing science he was researching. For example, Tony learned about gene therapy, the technique of treating diseases by inserting a gene into a patient's cells to replace a defective or mutated version, which was considered risky. Unfortunately, only a few gene therapy products had been approved by the FDA for clinical use in diseases, including certain blood cancers, an inherited form of blindness, and childhood spinal muscular atrophy. And gene therapy for ALS posed additional challenges, such as identifying which gene or genes to target, especially in the sporadic form of the disease.

Stem cell therapy was another area that offered great promise for developing a new generation of molecular medicines.

Tony learned that stem cells are specialized human cells that have the ability to develop into many different cell types, including blood, bone muscle, and even neurons. While he was familiar with the ethical issues of isolating embryonic stem cells from fertilized human embryos, which meant a human embryo would have to be destroyed, he was surprised to learn that, increasingly, the focus of ALS cellular research had shifted to something called induced pluripotent stem cells or iPSCs. These were a type of stem cell that was created in the lab from adult skin samples or blood cells, thereby eliminating the ethical considerations of preparing embryonic stem cells. Tony had read that scientists had already programmed iPSCs to convert to motor neurons in the lab. *Fantastic!* he thought to himself. *Wouldn't the replacement of dying neurons in the brain with new ones derived from adult stem cells represent an effective strategy for treating ALS?* Unfortunately, as usually was the case with ALS, this potential approach was plagued with many technical challenges, not the least of which was that, when injected into experimental animals, newly created neurons from the lab failed to make the proper connections, or synapses, between muscles and surrounding neurons. Essentially, they didn't work.

Perhaps the most promising treatment approach for ALS that Tony researched was an area that Dr. Gladstone had mentioned, neurogenesis, or the process of generating new neurons in the brain itself. Tony remembered the dogma he had learned in a high school biology class years ago; the adult mammalian brain is incapable of generating new nerve cells following the destruction of such cells by injury or disease. However, in recent years, repeated demonstrations of active, adult neurogenesis in many mammals, including humans, had laid this theory to rest. It turns out that a small population of neural stem cells exist in adults, and, under the proper conditions, these cells can transform into functional neurons and establish connections or synapses with other neurons. *This is it,* thought Tony. *A drug that can promote neurogenesis and restore functional neurons in ALS patients could be the golden bullet.* Unfortunately, Tony's research had failed to uncover any evidence for such a drug. Furthermore, even if such a compound were discovered, it would face the usual mountain of technical hurdles before it could be advanced as a treatment. For example, it would have to cross the blood-brain barrier, a sort of specialized security system that blocks the passage of many substances into the brain. Tony recalled reading somewhere that ninety-eight percent of potential drugs for brain disorders were unable to penetrate the blood-brain barrier. No wonder drug development in this therapeutic area was so challenging and unforgiving.

CHAPTER SIXTEEN

Although the bright sunlight pouring through the large glass window in his home office foreshadowed a clear day, Tony's mind was anything but unclouded. Yes, he had learned so much about ALS, including its pathology, progression and even its potential therapies. But he had failed in his major objective—uncovering an effective treatment for Ann. Even if a drug that promotes neurogenesis offered a glimmer of hope for her, how was he to uncover such an agent if, in fact, it actually existed?

Tony's studies were interrupted by a call from his sister, Karen, phoning to check on Ann. Tony briefed her on Ann's condition, then turned to the subject of his research.

"Remember those trips to the World's Fair we took as kids when the future seemed so bright? Back then, we had plenty of time to imagine a future with all those great technologies like video phones. But when the clock is ticking against you as it is for Ann, it's hard to get excited about a future that seems so obscure. That's how I feel when I search for new ALS treatments. Everything I read about is under development for use at some uncertain future date, and nothing is available that helps us now when we need it. And if there is something useful out there, I have no connections in the field to help me find it."

Karen answered, "Tony, you need some expert assistance.

When we need insights here at Morgan Stanley on some special topic, we identify professionals in that area and bring them in as consultants. You have to identify some experts in neurobiology and talk with them about the latest developments."

After a few more minutes, Tony ended the call with his sister and reflected on her advice. *She's absolutely right,* he thought. *For any chance of success of uncovering a promising new therapy, I have to get closer to the science and the scientists driving the drug discovery research. If anyone knows about a magic bullet under development, it would be the researchers working in the trenches at experimental laboratories.*

Fortunately, the ALS Association's website was a rich source for names and affiliations of leading scientists scattered across the country. In studying the listings, he identified James Cahill, a Ph.D. scientist who led the drug discovery efforts in the central nervous system area, commonly referred to as CNS, for Hopeton Pharmaceuticals, a multibillion-dollar pharmaceutical company located just outside of Philadelphia, about thirty miles from Tony's home. This local expert appeared to represent a reasonable starting point for Tony's investigations.

Tony reasoned that an unsolicited call or email to Dr. Cahill had a low probability of being returned; he needed some type of professional forum or assembly to introduce himself. Scrolling through the web pages of the ALS Association, he discovered that they were sponsoring a local chapter meeting in Philadelphia the following week to discuss clinical trial design and patient recruitment strategies. Tony knew that all new drugs had to be evaluated in clinical trials, and he imagined designing such trials for a disease as complicated as ALS could be a nightmare. No wonder an entire meeting was dedicated to the subject. Dr. Cahill was listed as one of the panel members and speakers for the one-day event. *Here is my chance,* thought Tony, as he hurriedly completed the online registration form. Local chapter meetings, such as this one, were usually free for patients and their family members.

The following Tuesday morning, Tony joined the harried flock of commuters driving to Philadelphia on the busy 95 Interstate and navigated through the city's downtown area, commonly referred to as Center City, that encompassed the city's cultural, tourist, and economic hub. Driving down Broad Street, littered with trendy hotels, bars, and restaurants, he arrived at the Doubletree Hotel, the venue for the day's conference. He parked his five-year-old Subaru Outback in the hotel's underground garage, noticing a disproportionately large number of expensive Mercedes, BMWs, and Lexus models. *They must cater to an exclusive clientele here,* he thought. Reaching the main lobby, he spotted a sign directing meeting participants to the Eagle Conference room on the second floor. He rode an escalator up one flight and approached a table bearing a large sign proclaiming REGISTRATION.

A young man sitting behind the table asked, "Are you pre-registered?"

"Yes," responded Tony. "My name is Anthony Lucas."

"Okay. Here we are," responded the man as he handed Tony an ID badge proclaiming Anthony Lucas/Guest and a short program booklet listing the day's agenda. "The meeting will start in ten minutes. Lunch is provided next door in the Sun Room."

"Thanks. Could you identify Dr. James Cahill for me? I wanted to catch up with him before the sessions started."

"Sure. See that tall gentleman with the blue blazer and gray pants standing next to the table? That's Dr. Cahill."

Tony thanked the man and strode purposefully towards a long, linen-covered table displaying breakfast fare of bagels, danish, and a large coffee urn. A number of attendees were huddled in line for the treats while the man identified as Dr. Cahill stood off to the side, sipping a cup of coffee and staring intently at his iPhone. Briefly studying him from a few feet away, Tony sensed that the tall, neatly dressed man exuded a certain aura of confidence. Tony approached him and said, "Dr. Cahill. My name is Tony Lucas, my wife has ALS, and I'm very interested in talking to you about new treatments that you may be aware of, either at your company or elsewhere."

Dr. Cahill was gracious in his response, especially considering the fact he had never met Tony. "I'm sorry to hear about your wife. ALS is a heavy burden, to say the least, and it can be very difficult to treat with the limited drugs at our disposal. I'd be happy to discuss some programs under development. Let's meet during the lunch break. I see the morning sessions are just about ready to start."

"That would be great. Thanks so much. I'll meet you back here at noon."

Tony followed Dr. Cahill into the adjoining conference room and took an aisle seat near the front. As he listened to the various talks and discussions over the next few hours, the fervor expressed by most of the participants affected Tony on a personal level. Whether they had a direct connection to ALS or not, all the speakers and panelists left the impression that helping ALS victims had become their life's mission. Tony took solace in the realization that he wasn't alone in his fight.

As the conference adjourned for lunch, the attendees were directed to the adjacent conference room. Tony entered this room and noticed a layout with multiple circular tables, each containing many chairs and place settings. He grabbed a seat at the foremost table, and as Dr. Cahill entered the room, gestured to him.

As Dr. Cahill took his seat, Tony started. "Excellent sessions, Dr. Cahill. I learned so much. And you did a great job in moderating all those panelists. Each one seemed to have a different opinion on where the research is heading."

"That's usually the way it is with these things," answered

Dr. Cahill. "There is so much work going on that it's challenging to hear everybody's perspective in an hour. And by the way, please call me Jim."

"Thanks, Jim. I appreciate that, and also your taking the time to meet with me."

Over the next several minutes, they exchanged some details on their personal and professional lives before Tony launched into a detailed description of Ann's situation. As their discussions continued, Jim's modest and easy-going nature impressed Tony such that he felt a real connection form between them. Like Tony, he had grown up in Brooklyn and was a lifelong Yankees fan. This Yankees connection never ends, thought Tony. Following the completion of a doctoral program at Yale, he had spent a few years doing postdoctoral research in neurology at the prestigious Salk Institute in San Diego. He then joined Hopeton Pharmaceuticals, where he had risen in the ranks to become the leader of their CNS research group, a cluster of over fifty Ph.D., MD, and BS level scientists engaged in discovering novel therapies for serious neurological diseases, including ALS.

What an impressive background, thought Tony, as he imagined the logistical and technical challenges of directing a team that large.

When asked about potential treatments for the disease, Jim spent several minutes reviewing over a half dozen drugs in various stages of development at different companies and their mechanisms of action. Tony was familiar with some of these targets that included gene therapy and stem cells, while other approaches such as blocking pro-inflammatory molecules called cytokines, inhibiting calcium release, and increasing copper ion uptake were foreign to him. Jim also reviewed the strategy his company was using to target ALS. It involved blocking one particular gene implicated in certain forms of the familial ALS with a small piece of DNA referred to as anti-sense.

Tony asked, "Could any of these potential approaches lead to drugs that cure the disease, especially the sporadic form?"

Shooting him an understanding glance, Jim responded, "Not likely. Most of the drugs in development were designed to reduce symptoms, not cure the disease. Furthermore, ALS is an extremely complex disorder, probably due to a combination of different neurological factors. We are just now realizing how variable ALS is from one patient to the next, and specific treatments that are effective in one subset of patients may be virtually ineffective in another."

Tony responded, "How about a neurogenesis agent that promotes the growth of new neurons to replace those destroyed by the disease? Is there anything going on with that approach?"

"That type of agent would be revolutionary," declared Jim. "In theory, it could reverse at least some of the symptoms of ALS in all types of patients. At Hopeton, we follow the latest research in neurogenesis, and unfortunately, I haven't heard of any such agent."

As a bell sounded calling attendees back for the conference's afternoon sessions, Tony said, "Thanks again for meeting with me and providing the wealth of information. It really means so much to me, although it doesn't look like there is anything out there that will make a real difference for Ann."

"Sorry I couldn't have better news for you," replied Jim in his gracious manner. "I wish you and your wife the best. Here's my business card. Feel free to call me with any additional questions you may have. And if you give me your number, I'll be sure to call if I hear about any new developments that could help Ann, especially in the area of neurogenesis."

As Jim walked away, Tony felt a range of mixed emotions. On the one hand, he was amazed at the dedication of scientists across the globe who were boldly investigating exciting, novel approaches to treat ALS. He had no idea that so many drugs were in the ALS pipeline. However, on the other hand, every potential approach they had discussed was new and untested, and all were designed to ameliorate and not cure the disease. And even if some novel drugs were available for patients in the not-too-distant future, would any of them be available in time to benefit Ann, whose condition was rapidly deteriorating?

CHAPTER SEVENTEEN

Tony returned home later that afternoon and immediately checked in with Ann to update her on his meeting. By now, she was mostly wheelchair-bound and barely capable of taking even a few steps unaided. Tony also noted an increase in the shortness of her breath; he knew this was one of the symptoms of ALS. He wondered how long before she would lose her ability to speak, eat, or perform any activity under voluntary muscle control. His window of opportunity for finding an effective treatment was rapidly closing, and in spite of his increased knowledge about ALS, he was no closer to finding a cure for Ann than when she was first diagnosed several weeks ago.

Trying to paint an optimistic scenario, Tony said. "I learned so much today. There are research groups all over the world exploring new treatments for ALS. It's just a matter of time before something new comes along that will really impact this disease."

Ann smiled weakly and responded. "I'm glad to hear that. But you know as well as I do that time is not on my side."

Tony gulped as his throat constricted, trapping his breath in his lungs. Unable to speak, he could only manage a slight nod in agreement. Ann's stark words had perfectly summarized the grim reality.

Over the next few days, a new sense of desperation set in as he began to fully appreciate the futility of his pursuit. The more he learned about ALS, the more improbable it seemed that a cure for Ann existed.

The dire situation reached its nadir two days later when Tony discovered Ann sprawled on the dining room floor, flailing helplessly. She had fallen out of her wheelchair and was incapable of getting up by herself. Tony rushed to her assistance, and speaking soft words of encouragement, gently lifted her back into her seat. *My poor Ann,* he thought. *How could it come to this?* On the spot, he recommitted to supporting her in every possible way until the bitter end, whose approach seemed like a hopeless, foregone conclusion.

A few days later, Tony was working from his computer, continuing his online research. Most of his efforts had now shifted to investigating the best approaches to caring for patients with advanced ALS rather than exploring potential treatments. *I guess I failed in that mission,* he thought, recalling his earlier vow to leave no stone unturned in finding a cure for Ann. He turned back to glance at the web page that described the bleak details of late-stage ALS, when he noted a link to an article titled "Environmental Causes of Sporadic ALS." From his earlier research, he was familiar with the theory postulating that certain environmental toxins may cause some forms of ALS. However, none of the many papers he had read on the subject had provided any relevant information concerning new treatments. Out of habit, he haphazardly clicked on the link to open the new page. An article appeared that described how, after World War II, military doctors in the Pacific island of Guam observed that, over several years, many natives had developed symptoms similar to ALS. Some physicians speculated that this unusually high disease incidence was due to the ingestion of local shellfish contaminated with a certain type of bacteria termed cyanobacteria. *Interesting,* thought Tony as he reminded himself of Ann's lifelong love of shellfish, from her childhood days growing up near the coastal waters of lower Delaware to her life with Tony where she enjoyed every available raw oyster bar offered by restaurants when they dined out. *Could Ann's shellfish consumption over the years be the reason she developed ALS?*

As he continued reading, Tony suddenly froze in his chair as he noticed a short sequence of letters in the article—B-M-A-A. He thought, *I know that sequence.* Squeezing his eyes shut, he took a deep breath and searched the far reaches of his memory. As he tried to recall the specifics, he opened his eyes and read that BMAA was an acronym for beta-methylamino-L-alanine, a neurotoxin produced by cyanobacteria. It came to him in a flash! He bolted out of his chair and rushed upstairs, searched the back of his closet, and grabbed the rusted old safe that hadn't been opened in years. The combination of nineteen and five came to him instinctively. *How ironic,* he thought. *I can remember certain things from childhood over fifty years ago clearer than events of just yesterday.* Spinning the dial to enter the combination, he opened the safe and grabbed a yellowed piece of folded loose-leaf paper. Unfolding the page, he anxiously read the still visible words printed in the large blocks letters that he had penciled in from memory all those years ago: MIRACLE CURE FOR CRIPPLING DISEASE, DISCOVERY, GEORGE JANUSOWSKI, ALMED, BMAA-IN. There it was: BMAA. Astonished, Tony sat cross-legged on his bed as his mind raced at warp speed. Could these few words from his past actually provide a real connection to the current situation? Was the BMAA of the article the same neurotoxin he had just read about? And, if so, what did the -IN at the end of BMAA signify?

Tony recalled that most of the print from that article had been illegible due to the smeared ink. Reasoning that IN was probably the beginning of a word whose remaining letters had disappeared, he began a mental exercise of trying to form words by filling in possible, missing letters after the IN: included, incapable, increased, incredible, investigated. On and on he went, but nothing made sense to him. *Wait a second,* he thought. *If the article was describing some crippling disease, and BMAA is a potent neurotoxin that causes a disease, perhaps the IN could be the start of induced, for BMAA-induced. That's got to be it,* reasoned Tony excitedly. And if the crippling disease of the article was BMAA-induced, then that disease could very well be ALS. He then reread the headline he had scribbled all those years ago, focusing on those crucial words: MIRACLE CURE!

Over the next several minutes, Tony's emotions ranged from the peak of hopeful elation to the trough of doubtful despair as he carefully considered his nascent hypothesis. So many questions ran through his mind. *Could this fragmented newspaper story actually be telling me there may be a cure for ALS out there, somewhere? But even if I am correct in my theory, how can I locate a cure that won't be reported until 2025, seven years in the future? Or is this tenuous connection to ALS and is a possible remedy for Ann's desperate plight merely wishful thinking? Is my desperate hope for a cure causing me to fabricate a potential solution from fifty-year-old fragmented sentences and snippets of letters?*

Tony recalled that the other two headlines from that 2025 newspaper had already contained proven truths. The Yankees did collapse in the 1965 season, and Bill Clinton was elected President in 1992. This was too much of a coincidence to ignore. In his heart, he felt that the futuristic newspaper story was somehow linked to his current situation with Ann. Furthermore, since his research over the past few months had failed to uncover any prospects of a cure for Ann's disease, then this evidence, as dubious as it was, represented the only tangible lead he had.

With a renewed sense of determination, Tony carefully scrutinized his printed words from 1965 one more time.

MIRACLE CURE FOR CRIPPLING DISEASE, DISCOVERY, GEORGE JANUSOWSKI, ALMED, BMAA-IN. Crippling disease and discovery were terms that were just too general in nature to provide specific clues, at least at this stage of his investigation. He then considered ALMED. Was it the first part, or even the last part, of some word? Pulling out the old Random House Dictionary from the bottom shelf of his nightstand, he failed to discover any word in the English language that began with almed. A quick Google search turned up a few almed references, including that of a food and beverage retail franchise in Dubai. *Nothing there is even remotely related to ALS,* thought Tony. *Perhaps almed was part of someone's name or part of some place's name.* He temporarily abandoned this line of thinking with the idea of returning to it later, and turned to the most concrete clue, George Janusowski.

Obviously, this had to be a man's name, although it did seem unusual. Another quick Google search failed to identify anyone with that particular name; in fact, no Janusowski turned up. *So much for an easy solution,* he thought, as he mentally formulated a plan for locating information on a George Janusowski. Over the next several hours, he redirected his efforts to several online people search engines such as whitepages.com, dobseartch.com, peoplefinder.com, and any other relevant site he could locate. Nothing turned up. *Was the man a ghost?*

Tony paused to reconsider his search strategy. In the context of the scant details he had to work with, he reasoned that a person mentioned very early in a newspaper story would be a prominent player in that narrative. *The two most prominent roles,* thought Tony, *would be either the discoverer of the miracle cure or a patient who recovered from the disease.* Remembering that the newspaper article was dated April 1, 2025, still several years in the future, it would be almost impossible to identify an individual today who probably hadn't yet developed ALS. However, a scientist or doctor would probably have to spend years of specialized research before uncovering a major new discovery, such as a cure for a crippling disease. Therefore, assuming that George Janusowski was a scientist working in neurological research, and especially on ALS, represented one possible approach for trying to locate him because the search criteria would necessarily be restricted by focusing on this specific type of expertise.

Tony spent the next several days virtually glued to the computer in his home office, searching every website he could think of with possible ALS connections for a list of names that could include Janusowski, including various ALS Associations, neurological disease consortiums, pharmaceutical and biotechnology companies with CNS franchises, major research centers, and large university-associated hospitals. He searched Find a Doctor websites in case George Janusowski was a listed physician. He utilized specialized search engines that he had previously explored during his pursuit of ALS cures, this time focusing on individual names instead of potential therapies. These sites included PubMed, a free archive of over thirty million biomedical and life science journal articles in case a Janusowski had published some scientific papers; USPTO.gov., the United States Patent and Trademark Office, in case he had filed a patent application or been granted a patent for some invention; and ClinicalTrials.gov., a database of publicly and privately funded clinical studies conducted around the world, in case he was a study director of some clinical trial. Nothing turned up.

Next, he called his contact at Hopeton Pharmaceuticals, Jim Cahill, and explained that he was trying to identify an individual named George Janusowski who might be working on a new treatment for ALS. Although his request sounded a bit odd and was certainly short on specifics, Jim was his usual courteous self. After telling Tony he knew no one by that name, he suggested an additional strategy; searching the attendance rosters of different international ALS meetings that he had attended over the past several years in case Janusowski had been a registered attendee. Jim reported back to Tony a few days later with negative results. Disappointed in the results as he was, Tony nevertheless thanked him profusely for his efforts.

CHAPTER EIGHTEEN

Tony's unsuccessful efforts in tracking down George Janusowski literally drove him to his wit's end. Perhaps his assumption that Janusowski was the discoverer of a miracle cure for ALS was erroneous. Or perhaps the man with the strange name was untraceable because he resided in some remote location or country. *Is this the end of the trail?* Tony thought, *at least if a few words and letters from a futuristic newspaper could be considered a trail?* As he mulled over this dismal possibility, Ann slowly rolled her wheelchair into his office and struggled to speak.

"You've been married to that computer the last few days. Have you discovered something useful?"

It pained Tony to no end to witness the physical deterioration of this once literate and eloquent English teacher who now labored to formulate and speak even the simplest sentences. As he prepared to answer his wife, it suddenly occurred to him that he had never shared his boyhood story of the key and the newspaper headlines with her, or in fact with anyone, first because of his fear that they would think he was a bit wacky, and then because the story had started to fade from his memory over the passing years. *Now is finally the time,* he thought. During their entire marriage, Tony and Ann had always worked as partners in dealing with every important issue they faced, whether it was related to family, finances, careers, or any other topic. *I owe it to her to tell her everything and explain why I am acting so obsessively. She deserves to know the truth, and perhaps she might even have an idea or two that hasn't occurred to me.*

He turned to his wife and began, "Let me tell you a story."

Over the next hour, Tony related the details of the bizarre tale from his boyhood, including the time capsule, the shimmering key with the strange two-faced icon, and the changing newspaper headlines. He told Ann how two of the futuristic stories, those concerning the Yankees and President Bill Clinton, were validated. He even ran upstairs to collect the old sheet of loose-leaf paper from his boyhood safe and showed her the words and letters he had printed all those years ago.

Continuing his story, he said. "And now I discovered that BMAA is an acronym for a toxin that may cause ALS. Those are the same letters I wrote down from the 2025 newspaper that referred to a miracle cure. It could all be a coincidence, but I think the disease in that article was ALS."

As he spoke these last words, Tony noted a spark in Ann's pale blue eyes, a glint that had been all but invisible since her diagnosis several months ago. Buoyed by this response, he continued. "The final words I wrote from that article were George Janusowski. This person could be the key to everything. I've spent the past few days trying to locate him, using every search engine possible. So far, I've got nothing."

Ann sat quietly in her wheelchair with rapt attention during the entire discourse. When Tony finished his saga, there were tears in her eyes, and she reached out her arms to hug him. "You did all that for me," she muttered in an almost inaudible tone.

Her words and actions melted Tony to his core as he felt his love for Ann percolate through him like a cooling ocean wave at the beach they loved to visit on hot summer days. After a minute, he recalibrated his emotions and continued. "I've reached a dead end. I can't locate a George Janusowski anywhere, and I'm not sure what my next step should be."

He was surprised to see that Ann was smiling at him. "Don't you see it?" she replied in her halting vernacular. "Your special aptitude for time is probably why you found the key, or more likely, why the key found you. That key unmasked those future stories to you and you alone. Like the time capsule containing newspapers from 1905 and 2025, it may very well represent the connection between your past and your future. If it is meant to help us through this ordeal, it will find a way for you to unravel the real meaning behind that newspaper article. If there is a solution to this ordeal, I believe the key holds it."

Tony carefully considered her words. She had provided a different perspective than his own, and as usually was the case with the various problems they had faced during their long marriage. By doing so, she had offered an alternate path to investigate possible solutions. He had been focusing his search on locating a George Janusowski; perhaps he would be better served by concentrating his efforts on uncovering information about the ancient key in an effort to unlock any secrets that might help them. He smiled; just one more example of why they made such a great couple.

Turning back to speak, he noticed her pained expression as she struggled to catch her breath with a series of shallow pants. Clearly, the exertions of the last hour had worn her out.

"Ann dear, as usual, you've given me a lot to think about. Now let's get you back in your bed."

He gently guided her wheelchair into the family room, where a rented hospital bed stood next to the large picture window overlooking their backyard. Ann used the window as her lens to the outside world that she could no longer directly experience. Tony helped her into the bed, wondering how much longer before it would become her permanent prison.

Following a short break to re-energize his mind, during which he munched on an apple and gulped down a can of sparkling water, Tony returned to his computer. *It's funny,* he thought to himself, *that in all the ensuing years since the eighth grade, I never once explored the origin of that key with the two-faced icon. Now is finally the time.* He proceeded to Google two-faced icon of ancient times and was immediately rewarded with multiple references to Janus, the ancient Roman god of time, who is usually depicted as having two faces since he looks to the past and the future. As a scholar of history, albeit American history, Tony felt somewhat abashed at his lack of knowledge of Roman mythology. Of course, he had heard of Janus before, but he never fully appreciated the connection between the deity and time. Clicking on one of the listed websites to open it, he viewed a rendering of a two-faced bearded man that resembled, as much as he could recall, the icon on the key he had found all those years ago. So, the key was made in the image of Janus and is probably a relic of ancient Rome. *At least that gives me a starting point for trying to find it or glean some information about it,* he thought.

While Tony was an expert in historical research, which relies primarily on written records and documents to interpret important lives and events, searching for an ancient Roman artifact like the key from his youth was a different matter. He reasoned the most logical starting point would be a museum with a large collection of pieces from that era. Another quick Google search identified the Metropolitan Museum of Art in New York City as the country's largest reservoir of such treasures, with over thirty-five thousand objects from Greek and Roman antiquity. He had visited the Met several times while growing up in Brooklyn but recalled his last visit was over twenty years ago when he had accompanied his daughter Monica during a school trip. Examining the artifacts on display at the museum would certainly be interesting but definitely not the most productive method for trying to identify a specific item such as a key, especially if it wasn't even on public exhibit. Perusing the Met's website, he located a listing of the various staff members. Under the Greek and Roman Collection heading, he identified the name of Ethel Warburg as chief curator. *If anyone can help me in this search, it has to be her.*

Tony deliberated on how to arrange a meeting with Ethel Warburg. Approaching her as a regular museum patron to ask a series of questions about a particular artifact would probably be futile. He thought, *What if I used my professional status?* He located the phone number for the Met, called the number, and, after what seemed an endless cascade of operators, was transferred to Ethel Warburg's voicemail. At the tone, he left a message. "Ms. Warburg, my name is Dr. Anthony Lucas, Professor Emeritus and former Chairman of the History Department at The University of Delaware. I am currently working on a book aimed at examining how the Roman Empire influenced the development of the United States democracy and would be extremely grateful if we could meet to briefly discuss specific questions on some Roman artifacts I have uncovered in my research. I actually have plans to be in New York early next week and would greatly appreciate it if we could arrange a short meeting at your office, schedule permitting. My number is 302-463-4444; I look very much forward to your reply. Thank you."

Now all I have to do is wait and hope for a response, he thought.

A few hours later, Tony's cell phone rang, and the screen displayed the Metropolitan Museum as the source of the call. Anxiously, Tony answered the phone and was pleasantly surprised to hear a woman's voice announcing herself as Ethel Warburg. Tony thanked her for the prompt response and briefly explained a few more fabricated details about his pending book. Following some general questions, she invited Tony to meet with her the following Tuesday afternoon at 3:30 p.m. in her office at the museum. Tony thanked her again for agreeing to see him and disconnected the call. *Well, step one is underway,* he thought. He felt a bit guilty about the false pretense of their meeting but reasoned it would be much easier to gather information from her if he omitted eerie details about future headlines describing miracle cures.

CHAPTER NINETEEN

The following Tuesday morning, Tony drove the short distance to the Wilmington Train Station and parked his Subaru in the nearby municipal garage. As with virtually every other expense, the daily parking fee in Wilmington was a fraction of the cost for a similar service in the Big Apple, one advantage of living in small Delaware. Tony crossed the street and entered the Joseph R. Biden Railroad Station, named in honor of the longtime Delaware senator and former vice president, who was a strong advocate of passenger rail. In 2009, then Vice President Biden announced a twenty-month restoration project funded in large part by a twenty-million-dollar infusion from the American Recovery and Reinvestment Act. As a result, the station had undergone many internal and external renovations to improve both its decor and its passenger accessibility. When the work was completed, the station was renamed in his honor. It always amazed Tony that the legislators and politicians who controlled the purse strings in Washington were usually the individuals honored by having important facilities, roads, and structures named after them. *How apropos in today's world,* thought Tony, *where most Washington insiders profited immensely from their offices, both during and after their tenures.* Tony remembered reading that more than half the members of Congress were millionaires. As an expert on early American history, Tony honored the concept of economic patriotism practiced by several early American politicians, who put the country's interest ahead of their own, often risking their own financial health in the process. *How would the Founding Fathers have viewed today's profit-making opportunity that serving the country had become?* He could only wonder.

Tony climbed the one flight of stairs to the rail platform and joined several other passengers in boarding the 12:10 p.m. Amtrak train shortly after it pulled into the station. Settling in for the ninety-minute ride to Penn Station in Manhattan, Tony reminisced about the many enjoyable trips he and Ann had taken to New York, whether to view a Broadway play, attend a baseball game at Yankee Stadium, or enjoy some other event. *I hope this trip proves productive,* he thought.

As the train rolled to a stop at its final destination in Manhattan, Tony exited and was literally carried along by the flow of people swarming towards the single exit way of a narrow staircase leading to the mezzanine level. Any concept of personal space was shattered as Tony involuntarily recoiled at every brushing touch from the surging stampede. He thought, *Couldn't someone devise a more civilized method for disembarking at America's most symbolic station? The 34th Street Station, which links Amtrak Rail with trains of the New York City subway, the Long Island Railroad, and the New Jersey Transit System, is the busiest passenger terminal in the United States, serving over six hundred thousand commuters daily.*

Walking through the subterranean labyrinth while dodging a maze of harried travelers rushing to and from their scheduled trains, Tony emerged from the station on Seventh Avenue, adjacent to the entrance of the famous Madison Square Garden. Relieved at his escape from the overcrowded, underground confines, Tony took a minute to compose himself as he scanned the brilliant blue horizon. *Not a cloud in the sky,* he thought. *Perfect weather, as if I could enjoy it.* He walked three blocks east to Madison Avenue and boarded the uptown MTA bus. Exiting at 82nd Street, he proceeded one block west to Fifth Avenue, the site of the major building of the largest art museum in the United States. The Met was the first museum along New York's famous Museum Mile, a stretch of Fifth Avenue between 82nd and 105th Streets, adjoining the tree-lined east side border of Central Park.

Tony took his place in the line forming on the huge granite steps leading to the museum's entrance. The steps, built in 1975, represented a destination themselves as a meeting place for all types of New Yorkers, and this afternoon was no different as several factions, including green economy advocates, anti-government protestors, and supporters of statehood for Puerto Rico, congregated in small groups at various points. Tony had arrived well ahead of his scheduled appointment so he could tour the museum's ancient Greek and Roman exhibition in advance of his meeting. He passed through the security checkpoint and entered the Great Hall, the museum's grand entry. Turning left, he followed a long hallway that displayed many large-scale sculptures from ancient Greece. At the end of the corridor, he entered the gallery labeled Greek and Roman Art.

Tony spent the next hour immersing himself in ancient Roman culture. While extraordinarily interesting, it proved a bit disappointing since no key rings or any references to such items were displayed. He then worked his way back to the main entrance where Ms. Warburg had said she would meet him.

Shortly after 3:30 p.m., he noticed a smallish, middle-aged woman approaching the security desk from one of the internal hallways and assumed she was his contact. He went up to her and asked, "Ms. Warburg?"

She nodded and replied in return, "Dr. Lucas?"

Following a brief exchange of pleasantries, she led him through what seemed like an endless maze of hidden doors and hallways until they reached a small, windowless office in the bowels of the building. Gesturing for Tony to take a seat, she asked him, "What can I do for you?"

As an expert scholar of American history, Tony knew that many of America's founding fathers, including George Washington, Thomas Jefferson, Samuel Adams, and James Madison, were enamored with the ancient Roman Republic, and he had no trouble formulating a hypothesis for his fictional book and explaining this to Ms. Warburg. Continuing his charade, he then disclosed the major reason he wanted to meet with her. "In my research, I uncovered a story that suggested a mysterious Roman artifact may have influenced one of the communal authors of the United States Constitution, Thomas Paine. Apparently, it was a bronze key attached to a finger ring. The key's shaft was carved in a two-faced image of the Roman god of time, Janus. According to some stories, this key had some strange properties in terms of predicting future events, and such properties may have influenced Thomas Paine. I came here today to see if you could provide any additional information on such a key, perhaps even its location."

As expected, Ethel Warburg was a treasure trove of information on the Roman Republic. She explained that the ancient Romans were the first civilization to make and use keys that were very similar to modern ones. They had also devised the innovation of a combination ring and key of the type Tony described. This style of key was used for all kinds of jewelry boxes and also for locks on strong boxes that were essentially storage chests for important documents, household goods, and precious gems in prominent Roman households.

"It is reasonable to assume that this key you describe was designed for such a strongbox in one of Rome's upper-class homes or domi," she offered. "Studying archaeological artifacts can often provide clues about the lives and, in certain cases, even the identities of individuals and families that owned and utilized such items. However, in this instance, there just aren't enough details to provide any specific information about this artifact or its original owner, and unfortunately, I have no first-hand knowledge of a Janus key of the type you described. Curiously though, I have heard stories of mysterious powers attributed to similar types of artifacts from ancient Rome. Without concrete proof, I generally discounted such stories as nothing more than myths."

Tony squirmed uncomfortably in his seat as he debated whether or not to relate his tale of the key and its inexplicable effects on the newspaper headlines. However, before he could decide, she offered up additional information.

"While I can't help you with any specific information about the existence and possible location of such a key, I can refer you to a colleague of mine who has spent his career studying specific relics of the Roman Republic, including keys. If anyone can help you in your search, it would be he."

Excitedly, Tony took the name and contact information of Peter Saxon, a Professor of Ancient Antiquities at Harvard University in Boston. Following a few more short exchanges about ancient Roman history, Tony thanked Ms. Warburg for her time. She, in turn, wished him good luck with his search and his book and then escorted him back to the Great Hall of the museum, where they shook hands and parted ways.

On the train ride back to Wilmington, Tony mulled over the information from Ethel Warburg. While disappointed that the specified key was not identified or located, he felt a bit of optimism in that at least she had heard stories of mysterious powers associated with certain Roman artifacts. He also had a new lead to pursue, Professor Peter Saxon of Harvard University.

When he arrived home, he found Ann sitting in her wheelchair in front of the TV and briefly reviewed the substance

of his meeting with Ethel Warburg.
"What next?" she asked.
"I guess I'm Boston bound."

CHAPTER TWENTY

The next day, Tony proceeded to duplicate the routine he had used to arrange his meeting with Ethel Warburg. After locating Peter Saxon's phone number from the online Harvard directory, he called and left a voice message detailing his meeting with Ethel Warburg and her suggestion that he meet with Tony to assist him with a historical book, and specifically, to discuss a mysterious key from ancient Rome that may have influenced one of America's Founding Fathers. The following day, Tony received a call from Professor Saxon; they spoke briefly but cordially, and he invited Tony for a visit at his Boston office in two days, Friday at 1:00 p.m.

"It's a lucky thing you caught me this week," he told Tony. "I'll be leaving next Monday for a month-long seminar series in Eastern Europe."

"Thanks for the invitation," replied Tony. "I look forward to meeting you."

On Friday morning, Tony was readying to leave for the airport to catch his short flight to Boston. In Ann's current condition, he was reluctant to leave her alone for any appreciable length of time. Andrew said he would be free to stop by around noon and stay with his mother until Tony returned from Boston later that day. However, Tony's flight was earlier in the morning;

therefore, he had asked his next-door neighbors and friends, the Logans, to stop by and stay with Ann until Andrew arrived.

As he was waiting for the Logans to appear, Ann slowly approached him in her wheelchair. Noticing her somber face, he met her gaze with a sympathetic smile and asked, "Why so down today?"

Ann mumbled in return, "I'm running out of time; I can feel it."

Indeed, Tony had noticed that her condition had appreciably deteriorated in just the past week, including increased dysphagia, or difficulty in swallowing, a decrease in her weight, and greater difficulty in articulating even the simplest of words. *How long before she will require a feeding tube just to stay alive?* he thought morbidly to himself.

He hugged his wife and responded to her in a more confident tone than he actually felt. "I think this trip could be our turning point. You know about my sixth sense of time; well, it's signaling me now that something good is about to happen."

A knocking at the door signaled the arrival of Tom and Nancy Logan. Tony escorted them into the living room and spoke. "Thanks again, Nancy and Tom, for coming over. I really appreciate it. I'm sure Ann will be fine for a few hours; I just feel so much better knowing someone is with her. She's in the family room with the TV on. Andrew will be here by noon. If you have any questions or concerns at all, don't hesitate to call me, or if I'm in the air, Andrew. Our cell numbers are listed on the side of the refrigerator."

Nancy replied, "Oh, it's no problem, Tony. Tom and I are glad to help out. We'll be fine." With those parting words, they made their way into the family room to join Ann.

Tony bolted out of the house and raced down the interstate in his Subaru, arriving at the airport in a little over twenty minutes. Wilmington's proximity to the sprawling Philadelphia

International Airport was a real advantage for harried travelers. He parked his car and joined the interminable line of anxious passengers at the security checkpoint in Terminal B. Waiting to clear security at airport terminals was one of Tony's least favorite activities, and he was certain many of his fellow passengers felt the same way. Ever since the 9/11 disaster, it seemed as if clearing the security line at the airport often took longer than the flight itself. He suspected that many of the policies enforced by the TSA were akin to closing the barn door after the cows had already exited. Did anyone really believe that the feeble, ancient-looking woman in front of him, who was currently being patted down by one of the agents, was attempting to smuggle a bomb on board her flight? As Tony inched his way forward on the line, he wondered if any of the policymakers had ever bothered to calculate the lost time and productivity such lines caused, let alone the emotional turmoil they induced in so many people worried about missing their flights.

When he was finally cleared to proceed to the departure gate, he barely had time to grab a Diet Coke from a nearby vending machine before boarding the plane. During the flight to Boston, he thought about Ann and her sense that their time together was running out. For the umpteenth time since her diagnosis, he cried silently to himself thinking, *How could it end like this?* Both he and Ann were practicing Catholics who had relied on their faith during their entire lives and strongly believed that their major purpose on earth was to improve the lot of others. However, in their current situation, it was difficult to ponder anything deeper than Ann's heartbreaking condition. He thought, *This Boston trip has got to pay off!*

After landing in Boston's Logan Airport, Tony grabbed a taxi to the Harvard campus and made his way to Boylston Hall, the home of Harvard University's Department of Classics in Cambridge. It was a beautiful, early spring day, and Tony felt suddenly bolstered by the bright sunshine, the warm-blowing breeze, and the bright, colorful foliage on the surrounding trees of the celebrated campus. He knew that the University of Delaware campus, where he had worked for so many years, was loosely modeled in the image of Harvard's campus. *That could be a fortuitous sign,* he thought to himself.

Entering Boylston Hall, Tony navigated his way to Peter Saxon's office, where he was met by a small, elderly man clad in a tweed suit and bow tie and bespectacled with pince-nez eyeglasses. Although Tony was, of course, familiar with the realm of academia, having spent his entire career there, he couldn't picture anyone who better epitomized the university world than the diminutive man standing in front of him.

After polite introductions, they sat down in Professor Saxon's cramped office, and Tony began to describe the reason for his visit. As with his earlier meeting with Edith Warburg at the Met, he decided to use the ruse of a potential book describing the influence of the Roman Republic on the American Founding Fathers to drive the discussion and keep his personal experiences with the ancient key to himself. Following a short overview of plans for his fictitious book, he turned to the topic of the key, describing its appearance to the best of his memory, as well as its alleged mystic power of shifting time. "Do you know anything about such a key?" he asked.

At the mention of the key, Professor Saxon had grown visibly more attentive and excited. "How fascinating that you uncovered rumors of such a key during the early days of the American Republic. Ironically, a key with a similar type of strange powers was reported to exist during the late stages of the Roman Republic. Years ago, when I heard an account of this mysterious key from an archivist at the Palazzo Massimo in Rome, I became so fascinated that I wrote my own notes on the story. Let me see where I placed those notes."

Standing suddenly, he turned toward the oversized, oak bookcase that hugged the wall in one corner of the small room. Its shelves literally heaved under the weight of books and folders, apparently aligned in no particular order. Prof. Saxon spent several minutes rummaging through several folders before exclaiming in a victorious shout, "Ah, here it is!" Pulling out a crumpled piece of paper etched with scribbled words in bold red ink, he proceeded to relate to Tony the major details from his personal notes.

"Apparently, an anonymous, private collector from 19th century England leaked some astounding excerpts from an ancient Roman diary in his archives. Unfortunately, both the collector and his Roman journal have disappeared from history. However, the diary purportedly detailed the life of a Roman olive oil merchant sometime between 10 and 100 A.D. who sourced his olive oil from Spain, known then as Hispania. One particular passage referenced a key fashioned in the image of Janus, the Roman god of time, and its magical power. By revealing terms of a future contract with a particular banker, it steered the merchant to a new source of funds that literally saved his enterprise at the last possible minute. The key somehow prophesied this financial solution before it actually occurred. In his diary, the merchant recorded that the key emitted a strange beam of light at certain times, and he specifically referred to it as, 'a key that predicted and changed the future as it guided me on a journey of chasing time.'"

Tony sat paralyzed during this revelation. The parallels between his own experiences and that of the Roman merchant were uncanny. In both cases, the keys had apparently altered or added text in a document, whether it be the newspaper from 1905 or the Roman merchant's contract with his banker, to predict future events; the keys were sculptured in the image of Janus and emitted beams of light from one set of Janus's eyes, apparently to indicate they were manipulating time; and, strangely enough, olive oil seemed to have played a central role in both situations. Tony recalled how he had found the key among the empty olive oil cartons in front of Louise's Italian restaurant. *This has to be the same key in both circumstances,* he thought to himself.

Turning towards Professor Saxon, he asked in an agitated tone, "Where can I find this key now?"

Momentarily startled at the stern tenor of Tony's question, he replied that he had no clues as to the key's whereabouts. "As far as I know," he continued, "the key hasn't been seen since the days of the Roman merchant who wrote about it in his diary. That's why your story of the Founding Fathers is so interesting; perhaps the key has survived over the years. Many ancient Roman keys were made largely of bronze, which is a corrosion-resistant metal, and have endured until today."

Tony knew it had survived; he had found this very key back in 1965. Anxious to learn as many details as possible about this story, Tony continued his questioning, "Can you tell me anything else about this Roman merchant?"

"Not many additional details are known about this man," answered Professor Saxon, "except that his name was Lucius Marcus Antonius, and according to one of his diary entries, he was obsessed with time."

At this disclosure, Tony blanched. The striking similarities between this Roman merchant and himself kept growing, even extending to their names, which were essentially mirror images of one another; Anthony Lucas and Lucius Antonius, and to their mutual fascination with time.

While Tony was considering these eerie coincidences, Professor Saxon started interrogating him about the sources that tied such a key to the early days of the American Republic. He explained the importance of verifying such sources so as to lend credence to the stories from the unknown nineteenth-century

British collector. Tony was purposely vague in his responses, once again opting to suppress any details about his own experiences with the key.

After a few more minutes, Professor Saxon excused himself. "I'm sorry to cut this meeting short. It's a fascinating subject. Any evidence suggesting that such a key is real, let alone that it may have impacted some historical events, would be extraordinary. However, I'll be leaving for Europe on Monday, and I have my last lecture in ten minutes. You can understand the importance of meeting with my class and my teaching assistants to make sure all is in order before my trip."

Tony replied, "Of course I understand. Thank you so much for seeing me on such short notice and for sharing the amazing tale of the Roman merchant and his key. Do you have any ideas on where I may find additional information about this story?"

"Unfortunately, no. My original source at the Palazzo Massimo passed away several years ago. As far as I know, the trail is a dead end."

With those words, Prof. Saxon rose to shake Tony's hand, and both men promised to contact the other if they learned any new details about the key or the Roman merchant.

Tony left Boylston Hall and spent several minutes wandering around the Harvard campus, lost in his thoughts and barely noticing the passing parade of students. What he had just learned was incredible! Somehow, he and this merchant from ancient Rome, both of whom shared common experiences and characteristics that were too striking to be coincidental, were linked by this mysterious key. Moreover, this key had helped Lucius Antonius overcome his contractual problems; could it also aid Tony with the challenge of solving Ann's ALS?

His excitement over this possibility started to wane as he realized that, in spite of this extraordinary new information, he was no closer to discovering the key or interpreting the unknown words and letters in the newspaper article than he had been before his meeting with Peter Saxon.

Tony caught a cab back to the airport and boarded the plane for his return flight to Philadelphia. Pondering these latest revelations during the trip home, he tried to formulate a strategy for moving forward. Unfortunately, he drew a blank. After visiting the leading American museum of ancient artifacts and personally meeting with two of the foremost experts on ancient Roman culture, what else could he do? Peter Saxon believed that the trail for the ancient key had disappeared centuries ago. And, although olive oil appeared to represent a common theme in their stories, how could Tony possibly utilize this information in his search? With no clues as to the key's whereabouts and with no more human sources to contact, he felt deflated. *What am I going to tell Ann?* he thought.

CHAPTER TWENTY-ONE

Following his deplaning in Philadelphia and drive home to Wilmington, Tony entered his living room and observed Andrew sitting on the sofa and reading a magazine. "How is your mother?" he asked anxiously.

"It's been so quiet, dad. Mom has hardly uttered a single word, and she never even stirred from her bed all afternoon. She has no energy at all. I hate to be morbid, but I think we all better start preparing for the end. Perhaps you should just plan on staying home from now on."

"I don't have any more travel plans. Why don't you get back to Mary and the kids now? Thanks again for coming over."

They hugged each other, and Tony bid his son goodbye. He then entered the family room, where Ann was lying in her bed. "Are you awake?"

She struggled to turn her head to face him and stammered in return, "Yes, how was your trip?"

Tony spent the next several minutes describing his meeting to Ann, who listened quietly with a curious expression on her face. When finished, Tony exclaimed, "Your suggestion to focus on the key was a smart one, and it led me to uncover this new information about the Roman olive oil merchant. It's amazing how similar our stories are, and the key is the common link. However, now it seems like a dead-end trail. I don't have any more clues to pursue. I'm so sorry."

Ann struggled to sit up in her bed and started speaking in her faltering voice. "You did everything you could; don't ever forget that. Perhaps the key doesn't want to be found just yet. I still believe that if it's meant to get a message to us, it will find a way to do so."

With her energy sapped just from the mere act of talking, she sunk back into her bed. Tony watched her forlornly as he contemplated her words. *She's probably right,* he thought; *it seems out of our hands now.* While he reluctantly agreed with her reasoning, it didn't alleviate the feelings of disappointment and sadness at his failure to help his wife with her torturous disease.

The following Monday, Tony drove Ann to Dr. Gladstone's office for her latest appointment with the neurologist. Dr. Gladstone took this opportunity to explain additional details on the progression of ALS and where Ann stood on this spectrum.

"Early-stage ALS, which Ann has already experienced, is characterized by muscle weakness, usually in the hands, arms and legs. During the middle stage of ALS, muscle weakness spreads to other parts of the body. Patients develop problems with walking, swallowing, and speaking, although they generally maintain their mental and reasoning abilities. As ALS advances to the late stage, most voluntary muscles become paralyzed. During this stage, eating and drinking usually require a feeding tube, and breathing is assisted with a ventilator. Ann's disease has progressed much more rapidly than I had hoped since the initial diagnosis several months ago."

Turning to face her directly, he continued. "Ann, you are in the middle stage of the disease now, and based on your symptoms, I believe that you will enter the late stage very soon, probably in a matter of weeks."

Ann responded to Dr. Gladstone's discouraging words

with a silent shrug. Tony thought, she probably doesn't even have the energy to ask any questions or the hope that anything can alter the course of the disease.

Tony asked, "Is there anything we can do to prevent or delay that onset?"

"Unfortunately, no. ALS is so variable from patient to patient, and for whatever reason or reasons, Ann's disease is accelerating very rapidly."

"So what do we do?" asked Tony in a desperate voice. Inwardly, he felt like crying.

"At this point, I would recommend palliative care for Ann. As her paralysis becomes more pronounced, the physical demands on you and your family in caring for her will become very strenuous, to say the least. Palliative care will provide a team of specialists to manage Ann's symptoms. As I recall, Ann's primary care physician is Dr. Smith. He would work in partnership with the palliative team and oversee the various aspects of her treatment. As the ALS worsens, the team can guide you through the advanced care stage, including decisions about the use of artificial feeding and mechanical ventilation. I wish I had better news, but at this stage, palliative care is the best option."

Tony felt sick to his stomach. He had tried to brace himself in advance for some disappointing news, but he was in no way prepared to deal with the rush of despair at hearing Dr. Gladstone's somber prognosis. While his rational brain had at least recognized the concept that their future time together was tenuous at best, his emotional brain was nowhere ready to accept such a conclusion.

Tony thanked Dr. Gladstone and gently wheeled Ann out of his office and back to their car. The drive home was quiet except for one short exchange.

"I agree with Dr. Gladstone's suggestion," said Ann.

"Are you sure?" asked Tony.

Ann merely nodded her head in assent. Tony knew that Ann was worried about how the loss of muscle function would render her totally dependent on her family for even the most ordinary tasks, such as washing, dressing, and eating. And Tony still had to manage the household, with all of its associated duties, including making doctor appointments, paying bills, maintaining their home, and communicating with family and friends. As soon as they arrived home, he started making calls to start the process of forming a palliative team. It was like arranging hospice care for patients with terminal cancer.

During the next few days, Tony became so preoccupied with the detailed planning of Ann's care that he had little time to think about the ancient key or a potential miracle cure for ALS. Whenever such thoughts did enter his mind, he pushed them away and sadly reasoned that there really wasn't much more he could do to unravel the clues from the 2025 newspaper article. *Maybe someday I'll tell certain people the story of the key,* he thought, *but, for now, I plan to keep it between Ann and myself.*

CHAPTER TWENTY-TWO

One casualty of Tony's hectic schedule was his appetite. By now, Ann had such little desire for food that Tony often had to coax her into sampling even the slightest amounts at mealtimes. Between his efforts to get her to eat, his busy schedule in caring for her, and, perhaps out of empathy for his wife, Tony himself had little interest in eating, let alone in preparing meals.

Ann would continuously scold him. "I have an excuse for not eating," she would say, "You don't."

Actually, Ann had anticipated the problem of preparing meals; she had done most of the cooking during their marriage and knew that Tony was unlikely to develop a sudden culinary passion after all those years. Therefore, shortly after her diagnosis, in order to make sure that Tony wouldn't be nutritionally deprived, she had signed up with a local meal subscription service in Wilmington to have fully prepared dinners delivered directly to their home three times a week. Ever health-conscious, even in her debilitating condition, she had chosen a service that focused on wholesome meals prepared according to the so-called Mediterranean diet. This regimen, which apparently accounted for the low incidence of chronic illnesses such as cardiovascular disease and cancer in inhabitants of countries bordering the Mediterranean Sea, included meals low in red meat, sugar, and saturated fat and high in produce, nuts, and other healthful foods.

Tony had grown accustomed to the meal delivery schedule, so when the doorbell rang one afternoon that week, he ambled to the front to collect his dinner. As he opened the door, he spotted a bright red delivery van parked in front of his house with the company name, ROSA'S MEAL SERVICE, inscribed in large bold letters on either side of the truck. All prior deliveries had been made in a battered white van with much smaller print on its sides.

"New truck?" he casually asked the young delivery man.

"Yes, it just came in yesterday."

Tony turned back to view the truck and noticed some new phrases printed in small lettering on its side panels. They read, "All meals prepared with virgin olive oil from Spain," and below that, "Your time is our passion." Immediately he realized that these two statements referenced common links he shared with the Roman merchant from Professor Saxon's story—olive oil from Spain played a central role in both of their experiences with the ancient key, and the two men shared a passion for time. With both of these themes prominently displayed on the truck in front of him, Tony wondered if the phrases were meant as some kind of signal for him to resume his chase for Ann's cure or merely represented a strange coincidence. As he deliberated over the phrase "Your time is our passion," the words triggered a distant memory in the back of his brain; he knew he had seen them before.

"Who came up with those slogans on your truck?" he quickly asked the young man standing in front of him.

"That's from the boss; she always has bright ideas about marketing."

"You mean Rosa?"

"Yes."

Tony thanked him, collected his meal, and walked towards

the kitchen to store the food until dinner time.

Leaving the kitchen, he remembered Ann's comment from the other day that if the ancient key wanted to get a message to them, it would find a way to do so. *Was this new delivery van the message board?* His first instinct was that this idea was ludicrous; how could some phrases on a food delivery van be designed to deliver a specific message for him? But the more he mulled over the idea, the more he convinced himself that there was something special about those phrases. His own experiences, along with those of the Roman merchant, were too real to automatically dismiss anything that mentioned both Spanish olive oil and a fixation with time.

The following day, Tony called the number for Rosa's Meal Service and asked to speak with Rosa. After she came to the phone, Tony mentioned that he and Ann were customers and that he wanted to talk to her about Ann's diet considering her ALS. Rosa was very gracious and invited him to stop by her kitchen/ office space in downtown Wilmington later that afternoon.

At 2 p.m., Tony drove himself downtown and parked his car in one of the large municipal garages. Heading down one of Wilmington's major thoroughfares, Market Street, he walked past the towering buildings of the city's banking center. Wilmington used to be best known as the home of the DuPont company, once the world's largest chemical firm. However, after decades of shedding divisions and reducing its workforce, and finally merging with the Dow Chemical Company, DuPont's influence on Wilmington had drastically waned. While banking remained a major industry, the downtown area now had a more casual air to it with an influx of newer marketing, design, and other innovative companies.

Tony continued down one of the side streets and approached a building bearing a large sign proclaiming, ROSA'S MEAL SERVICE. He passed through the doorway and entered a large room filled with bulky, professional, stainless-steel equipment, including ovens, sinks, refrigerators, dishwashers, and various prep tables. The pungent aroma of assorted spices that were being utilized in preparing the day's meals almost overwhelmed him. *This must be the place,* he thought to himself. He noticed three women busily attending to various tasks at the prep tables and waited momentarily before calling out. "I'm here to see Rosa."

A small, dark-haired woman wearing a white smock, hair net, and disposable vinyl gloves turned towards him and answered, "I'm Rosa."

As she approached him, Tony noted her pleasant mannerisms, intelligent expression, and bright, piercing, raven eyes. Introducing himself, he reminded her that they had spoken on the phone earlier in the day.

"Of course," Rosa replied. "Just give me a minute to finish this dish, and then we can talk."

Tony watched with interest as Rosa proceeded to chop assorted vegetables and pour them into a large bowl containing pasta. She then added a large cup of yogurt, sliced olives, what appeared to be feta cheese, corn kernels, several large tablespoons of olive oil, and finally some salt and pepper. After mixing the bowl's contents with a large spatula, she covered it with plastic wrap and placed the bowl in one of the large refrigerators. "That's my creamy Greek salad pasta dish," she exclaimed to Tony as she removed her hairnet and gloves and proceeded to wash her hands at one of the large stainless-steel sinks. "Why don't you come back to my office, and we can talk?"

Tony followed Rosa through a side door and toward the back of the building, where several small rooms were located. Rosa beckoned Tony to enter one room containing a desk with a red upholstered task chair behind it and two contemporary, wooden chairs placed in front. As Rosa sat behind the desk, he positioned himself in one of the chairs facing her.

She started the conversation by introducing herself as Rosa Martini and then expressing sympathy for Ann and Tony. Rosa had learned about Ann's ALS several weeks ago from her employee who had spoken to Monica during one of his deliveries to their house. Rosa continued, asking Tony if there was any special food he would like her to prepare, especially as Ann's condition worsened and her ability to swallow food became more compromised. He gratefully acknowledged her concern, and they spent a few minutes discussing various food options that were easier to chew and swallow.

Rosa was an extremely solicitous individual, and Tony grew very comfortable in her presence as their conversation continued. When they finished planning Ann's diet, he started to gently probe with questions about the adages on her truck. "I noticed a new delivery truck yesterday, and I was intrigued by the phrases on it. Why Spanish olive oil? I thought the best olive oil came from Italy."

Rosa stirred in her seat as she enthusiastically answered. "Most people in America view olive oil as an Italian product because of its association with traditional Italian cuisine. However, Italy has to source much of its olive oil from other countries since its own internal production does not meet the demand for the product. A recent investigation found that about half of the Italian olive oil bottles contain products from another country. And the major other country is Spain. It turns out that Spain is the world's top olive oil producer, in terms of both quantity and quality. There is actually an organization called World's Best Olive Oils that ranks olive oils, and in recent years Spanish brands have dominated this listing with up to eight of the top ten spots. Since virgin olive oil is a staple of the Mediterranean diet that is our specialty, I am proud to promote Spanish olive oil in our branding. It's time that people learned the facts about Spain and its olive oil."

Rosa's story reminded Tony that the Roman merchant, Lucius Antonius, sourced his olive oil from Spain. Another strange coincidence! He continued his questioning. "How about that phrase, 'Your time is our passion.' Where did that come from?"

"Oh," she answered. "That's from my dad. Ever since I can remember, he always had a passion for time. He used to keep over twenty clocks running in our house where we grew up. My sister and I would often tease him about it, but that sixth sense of his really saved both of us on several occasions.

"How so?"

"Well, in one case, Nina, that's my sister, and I were scheduled to fly to Los Angeles to visit our aunt. Without any warning, this was in the days before computers and smartphones, Dad got both of us out of bed at 5 a.m. and rushed us to the airport so that we arrived several hours before our flight's scheduled departure. We kept on pestering him during the drive about leaving so early, but he wouldn't answer. Well, when we reached the terminal, we saw that our flight had been moved up by three hours, and we had barely enough time to board the plane before it departed, virtually empty, I might add. It turned out the Los Angeles area was expecting a huge series of thunderstorms, and all scheduled flights after ours were canceled for the day. I always marveled at how he knew our plane would be leaving early; he just told us he could sense it. He had a gift for predicting the timing of certain events. I don't know how he did it."

While Rosa was recounting her story, Tony felt his head pulsing as a diffuse picture started to form in the back of his mind. It was the image of a warm summer afternoon in a ballpark with its lush green infield and expansive outfield. He could sense the unmistakable aroma of hot dogs, mustard, and beer hanging in the air. Tony suddenly recalled when and where he had first seen that phase, "Your time is our passion." It was that day at the Orioles-Yankees game, some thirty-six years ago, when one of the co-winners of the contest drawing was wearing a T-shirt emblazoned with that same motto. In a flash, additional details came to Tony…the man's oversized wristwatch, his self-described fixation with time, his premonition that something important would happen to the Orioles at the game he had chosen for his prize, and his hurried departure to be with his wife and new baby daughter. He had to be Rosa's dad. That baby girl must now be the woman sitting across from him at this very moment!

Tony knew he had to speak to this man again. "Where is your dad now?"

Rosa gave him a pensive glance. "Dad passed away about two years ago, just a few months after my mother."

Tony felt personally devastated that this man, who had shared a unique ability with him and represented a potential source of additional information, was deceased. *My best chance to discover new clues that may help Ann just disappeared,* he thought to himself. Nonetheless, he managed to convey his condolences to Rosa on the loss of both parents.

Trying to glean as much information as he could about this man, he continued, "If you don't mind my asking, what was your dad's name, and what line of business was he in?"

"His name was Robert Arbore, and he owned an Italian Emporium in Baltimore. You know, the kind of store that sells Italian goods and foods."

Now Tony also recalled additional details from that summer day meeting, when the gentleman had, in fact, introduced himself as Robert and declared that he owned some type of specialty store in Baltimore. It all fit together.

"Was one of his products olive oil?"

Surprised at the question, Rosa replied that indeed his dad had sold olive oil. "It was his best-selling product; in fact, we import olive oil for our recipes from the same source Dad discovered. As I mentioned earlier, it's actually Spanish olive oil, but Dad would never tell his customers that. Everything had to be Italian for them. However, I believe it's time that Spain got its due, at least in terms of its olive oil."

All the similarities among Lucius Antonius, Rosa's dad, and himself, even extending to the specific country of origin for the olive oil in their stories, had to be more than mere serendipity. Taking a deep breath, he leaned a bit closer to Rosa and said," Rosa, you'll probably think I'm crazy, but I think there is a connection between your dad and my wife's battle with ALS."

She looked at him suspiciously and backed away in her seat as she replied. "I don't see how that's possible. As far as I can tell, my dad never even knew your wife."

"Rosa, if you have some time now, I'd like to try and explain, beginning with the fact that I once met your dad at an Orioles-Yankees baseball game some thirty-six years ago. That day we both won a drawing for tickets to a future game, and we wound up independently choosing the same date from over sixty possibilities. Furthermore, we discovered another common thread that day; a strange gift for predicting certain future events such as he exhibited when he foresaw the early departure of your flight to Los Angeles. Those striking parallels suggest more than simple coincidences were at play."

Tony could tell that his words had piqued Rosa's interest, especially at the mention of the Orioles game. She responded, "That makes some sense; my dad was a huge Orioles fan for as long as I could remember. Let's hear the rest of your story."

Tony spent the next several minutes describing the major details of his long saga, from his finding that strange key years ago, to the futuristic newspaper headlines that had been partially validated, at least concerning the Yankees and Bill Clinton, to the possibility that the letters BMAA-IN suggested the crippling disease of the headline was, in fact, ALS, and finally to the recent discussions with Professor Saxon and his story of Lucius Antonius. He proceeded to explain the eerie similarities between Lucius and himself—a special fascination with time, including the ability to predict the outcome of certain events, a time-bending experience where altered versions of established documents or papers foretold future events, probably due to the strange key with the Janus icon, and a connection with olive oil.

"And now we have established that your dad shared some of those same features with me; a passion for time, an ability to predict certain events, and an olive oil connection—Spanish olive oil to be more precise."

Rosa scoffed at this latest statement. "Your conclusion seems pretty farfetched to me. The time thing is probably just a coincidence, and your finding an old key by an olive oil carton is hardly a strong connection with olive oil."

"I know it sounds bizarre, but it must mean something that your dad and I crossed paths over thirty years ago, and here I am today, speaking to his daughter about those two common elements, time and olive oil. There has to be more to these encounters than chance meetings between strangers. I believe everything I told you this afternoon happened for a reason, and that reason may have something to do with your dad and the ancient key. If he encountered it sometime during his life, perhaps his story could help me in locating it and interpreting the message in that newspaper article, information that could save my wife. Did your dad ever mention a similar type of key to the one I described?"

Tony's growing hopes for learning new insights about the key were dashed upon hearing Rosa's terse response.

"No, he never mentioned such a key, at least not to me. And nothing like that turned up in his belongings that we rummaged through after his death."

He could tell by the tone of Rosa's response that she remained unconvinced about any special connection with her father.

"Look," she continued. "Your story is really quite remarkable in many ways, especially concerning those altered newspaper stories that you read as a boy. However, I just can't understand how my father could be involved, especially as he never mentioned a strange key, which, from all you told me, appears to be the vital piece that would link everything together." Rosa rose from her chair, signaling an end to their conversation. "I'm sorry, but I really must get back to my work. If I think of anything that might connect my dad to all of this, I'll certainly let you know. But for now, I don't see how I can help you."

Tony felt completely defeated. His last chance of somehow saving Ann by discovering new insights from this woman was shattered. As he rose to leave, Rosa noted the look of abject despair on his face, and out of sympathy, asked one more question—if for no other reason than to try and slightly assuage his disappointment before departing.

"You mentioned the letters BMAA may have been a clue for ALS; what were the other letters whose meaning you couldn't decipher in that article?"

Dejectedly, Tony responded, "The other letters I read were a-l-m-e-d; all I could find out from a Google search was a retailer from Dubai by that name."

Rosa immediately sat back down in her chair and asked Tony in a serious tone, "Did you say a-l-m-e-d?"

"Yes," replied Tony as he sensed a new, heightened level of interest from Rosa. "Why do you ask?"

"This may mean nothing, but the region where my father sourced his olive oil and where we still import ours, is from a family-owned olive farm in Almedinilla, a small Spanish city in the province of Cordoba. The 'almed' in your article could be the beginning of Almedinilla."

Tony felt the air escape from his lungs. Were the letters a-l-m-e-d the start of Almedinilla? It all made so much sense. Excitingly, he asked Rosa, "Did your dad travel there?"

"Oh, yes. When I was young, I remember he took a long trip to Europe to scout out new sources of olive oil. He had been importing olive oil from Italy, near the southern city of Lecce. However, a bacterial infection destroyed most of the olive trees near Lecce, drying up his supply. He then traveled to different regions of Italy and finally to Spain to investigate new sources. I don't know many specifics about his trip, except that he was away a lot longer than he was supposed to be. Mom was really getting anxious about his absence. And when he finally did return home, he couldn't say enough good things about Almedinilla and the Spanish olive oil he discovered there. He often told us that his expedition to Almedinilla was the strangest and most successful trip he ever took."

Hoping for some hint about the mysterious key, Tony anxiously asked, "Did he ever tell you why it was so strange?"

"No, he never did elaborate."

Tony knew that Rosa had to return to her work, so he hurriedly asked a few more questions. "Have you ever heard of George Janusowski? His name was cited in that 2025 newspaper article."

"No, I'm sure I would have remembered that name if I had."

"How about Almedinilla? Did you ever have the opportunity to travel there?"

"No. I certainly wanted to, and perhaps someday I will. But I've never been to Spain. However, I can provide the name and contact information for my liaison to the Reyes olive farm in Almedinilla where I source my olive oil. He is an Italian gentleman named Pietro Rossi. As I mentioned earlier, he knew my father. You may find it helpful to speak with him."

Rising to leave, Tony shook her hand warmly and said. "Thank you so much, Rosa. Your father's story and your insight on Almedinilla have provided new clues for me."

In turn, she handed him one of Pietro Rossi's business cards and spoke. "I wish I had more to tell you. Your story of the key is amazing. Please keep me updated on any new developments, especially as they relate to my father. If I think of anything else that may be useful, I'll let you know. And my best wishes for your wife's health. I truly hope you find a cure."

Tony nodded in assent and silently hoped there would be a future occasion to share some positive news.

Rushing home, Tony couldn't wait to share his latest findings with Ann. If he was correct about "almed" actually being the start of Almedinilla, then it represented another link between Rosa's dad and himself, and more importantly, perhaps, an important clue for unraveling the cryptic newspaper article about a cure for a crippling disease. Tony felt certain he was on the right track. He also knew his next trip had to be a visit to Almedinilla.

CHAPTER TWENTY-THREE

Tony's renewed optimism was dampened as he walked through the front door of his house and was immediately greeted by Judy Goodson, the visiting nurse provided by the palliative care program that Ann had enrolled in a few weeks earlier. The home service had been a helpful suggestion by Dr. Gladstone and now provided in-home visits by various specialists in addition to Judy, including a palliative physician, a physical therapist, a dietician, a speech pathologist, and even a chaplain all to attend to Ann's various needs. However, the somber expression on Judy's face spoke volumes about the nature of her intended words, and Tony gulped in anxious anticipation.

"Mr. Lucas," she began. "Ann's dysphagia is much worse now, and she is not achieving the proper nutritional requirements. While she still has adequate respiratory function, I think it's time that she has a feeding tube inserted to provide alternate access for foods, fluids, and medications. I have already consulted with other members of the palliative team, and we all agree that it's time. Now it's up to Ann to make the final call."

Tony asked, "Judy, would you describe the procedure to me, so I discuss it with Ann?"

Judy explained, "It's a relatively quick surgery involving the placement of an endoscope, a flexible tube with an attached camera, in the mouth, down the esophagus, and into the stomach. Next, the doctor would make a small incision in Ann's abdomen and insert a feeding tube through the opening. The camera aids the doctor in visualizing the stomach lining so the feeding tube can be positioned properly. Once the tube is securely fixed to the stomach wall, the endoscope is removed. Ann will probably receive an intravenous sedative and local anesthesia before the procedure, and the entire process should take less than an hour. The risks of the procedure are very low, with possible short-lived complications including difficulty in breathing, nausea from the medication, and pain at the insertion site. Importantly, the feeding tube will serve as a direct passageway for nutrients, liquids, and medications to reach the stomach, bypassing the mouth and the esophagus."

The image of Ann on a feeding tube sent shivers throughout Tony's body, another milestone event in her unrelenting descent into total helplessness. He thanked Judy for her detailed description and said he would talk it over with Ann.

Desolately he approached the family room where Ann was lying in her hospital bed. "Honey, I'm home." She struggled to turn her face toward him, and he almost toppled over from the trembling in his legs in response to the warm smile that greeted him. Tony started, "I have some very good news, but first, I need to talk with you about your nutrition." He proceeded to spin a positive story about the feeding tube, explaining its insertion as a trivial procedure and a simple solution that was necessary to assure that she achieved her proper nutritional intake. As he emphasized how the feeding tube would obviate the need for chewing and swallowing, he noted that Ann had started to cry. He felt awful, trying to imagine the horror and shame she felt as she processed this latest demoralizing news, and he had to hold back his own tears.

Ann weakly grabbed his hand in hers and whispered in

her raspy voice, "Never."

Tony had feared this would be her reaction, knowing Ann as he did. He continued. "Ann dear, you need to eat to maintain your strength, and you can't do it without this feeding tube. It's really not that big of a deal. Thousands of patients have feeding tubes inserted and live happy and productive lives."

Noticing the skepticism in her expression, he continued. "Before you make a decision about this, listen to what I found out this afternoon." Tony then described his meeting with Rosa, even exaggerating his level of excitement at the discovery of Almedinilla and its olive groves. "It all fits together, and just as you told me, if the key wants to get a message to us, it will find a way. Well, I believe it sent us this message, and now it's up to me to go and discover what that message really means. To do that, I have to go to Almedinilla and search for clues to a cure. But before I go, I need you to promise me that you will agree to the feeding tube and stay strong and positive until I return home."

Ann responded by gently squeezing his hand.

On Tuesday morning, Tony drove Ann to the local surgery center, where many outpatient procedures were performed. He assisted her with the check-in routine and stayed with her in the pre-op suite as the gastroenterologist who would be performing the procedure, Dr. Lankas, met with them briefly to review the procedure and ask if they had any questions. Tony then watched as two nurses wheeled her hospital bed out of the pre-op suite and down a brightly lit corridor toward a darkened room marked "Operating Room—Do Not Enter." The sight of Ann disappearing from view behind the closing doors of the shadowy operating room etched a chilling image in his mind. *Is this a one-way passage, and will I ever see her again?* he thought. Struggling to control his anxiety, he reminded himself that a gastrostomy was a relatively simple procedure and returned to the waiting room.

Approximately one hour later, Dr. Lankas reappeared to

inform Tony that all had gone well and that he could join Ann in the recovery suite. He sat with her there for almost an hour as a continuous parade of nurses shuffled in and out to monitor Ann's vital signs and also to explain in detail the use and care of the feeding tube. Tony was glad they had arranged the palliative home care service; it would make things so much easier for both. Ann's expression through the entire affair was one of resigned acceptance. Tony felt awful for her, but he knew this procedure was essential for assuring Ann's nutritional needs during his upcoming trip.

Tony planned to leave for Almedinilla the following Saturday. *How ironic is this? he thought. Spain has always been Ann's dream vacation spot, and here I am, planning to visit the country without her. Yet another cruel twist of fate brought on by her terrible illness.*

He knew Ann was apprehensive about his planned absence, and he found himself constantly reminding her how important the trip could prove in unraveling the mystery of the hoped-for cure. He spent most of the next few days organizing the details of Ann's care with the palliative staff, as well as finalizing his travel plans. He also briefed his children on his itinerary, telling them he was traveling to Spain to meet with a physician who had been advocating a new regimen to prolong the life of ALS patients.

Both Monica and Andrew strongly opposed his trip. "How can you leave Mom at this stage to chase some quack doctor in Spain?" asked Monica in a troubled tone.

Tony understood their frustration with him, but he assured them it was a necessary excursion and that he would return home as soon as possible. Silently he cursed himself for lying to his children.

On Saturday afternoon before departing for the airport, Tony found Ann in her customary position, resting on the hospital bed in their family room. As he started to speak, Ann began to sob and then spoke in her low, trembling voice, "I'm afraid I'll never see you again."

Tony hugged his wife and tried to console her. "I've got to do this, Ann, for both of us. I promise you I will return as soon as possible with information that will help us get through this. I promise!"

He then gave Ann one last hug, pronounced his love for her, and was emotionally tormented by the opposing forces tugging on his heartstrings—one directing him to a remote village in Spain, the other urging him to stay home with his distraught wife—turned away and left the room.

CHAPTER TWENTY-FOUR

Tony's flights to Spain were unremarkable. He flew from Philadelphia to Madrid, where he cleared customs and caught a connection for the ninety-minute trip to Granada International Airport. Officially known as Federico Garcia Lorca Granada-Jaèn Airport, in honor of the Spanish poet and playwright, it serves the province and city of Granada in the autonomous community of Andalusia in southern Spain. Granada is one of eight provinces of Andalusia, each one named for its capital city. Almedinilla, Tony's ultimate destination, was a small town of three thousand residents located in the neighboring province of Cordoba. Once Spain's poorest region, some of Andalusia's provinces now represented popular tourist attractions, thanks to their beautiful countryside, majestic mountains, and their hundreds of miles of coastline filled with sparkling, sandy beaches.

En route to Spain, Tony tried to familiarize himself with the area by reviewing some of its long history. He learned that in the epic struggle against Carthage, their ancient foe, the Romans, under the leadership of Scipio Africanus, invaded the Iberian Peninsula in 206 B.C. His army defeated the native Iberians and established Andalusia, then referred to as Baetica, as one of Rome's richest provinces. The area flourished under Roman rule for several centuries until the Vandals, and then the Visigoths overran the region in the 5th century A.D. In 711 A.D., Muslims crossed the Strait of Gibraltar from Tangier, now Morocco conquered the area and ruled for almost eight hundred years. During this period, the region's history was strongly dominated by the Moorish culture of North Africa. Today the legacies of both Roman and Moorish influences are still evident in the area's art, architecture, religious footprint, and literature.

Hoping to learn why olive oil was a recurring theme in the puzzle he was trying to solve, Tony also researched the olive trade of Andalusia. He discovered that olive trees had been cultivated for thousands of years and were an integral part of the Andalusian heritage, culture, and economy for most of its history. The warm, dry Andalusian climate and the tough, rocky soil make it an ideal location for olive groves. Surprisingly, the hearty olive trees produce better fruit and oil in poor soil than they do in rich fertile loam. During the Roman era, their galleys would sail up the navigable Baetis river, today known as the Guadalquivir, as far north as Cordoba, where they loaded various exports including minerals, salt, and, of course, olive oil for transit to Rome. This history reminded Tony of the Roman merchant Lucius Antonius, who secured his olive oil from southern Spain. He imagined that Lucius's galley must have traversed this same route up the Baetis River all those centuries ago during the voyage that rescued his enterprise.

Tony read that Roman demand for olive oil was so great that an artificial hill approximately one-hundred-fifty feet in height was created in Rome from the discarded ceramic jars, or amphorae, containing the imported olive oil, much of it from the Andalusian region. Known as Mount Testaccio, or Monte del Cocci—mountain of broken glass—this ancient dumpster site is estimated to contain remnants of over twenty-five million amphorae, each stamped with its own export date and the origin of the olive oil it once contained inside.

As Tony would have predicted, olive oil remains a vital component of the Andalusian economy. The region contains a massive expanse of some seventy-million olive trees, making it the largest tree plantation in Europe. In terms of annual yield, Spain produces over 1.7 million tons of olive oil, nearly double the amount of Italy. Three of Andalusia's provinces, Sevilla, Jaèn, and Cordoba, account for approximately two-thirds of Spanish production. Almedinilla was one of many olive oil-producing towns in Cordoba.

Through his readings, Tony developed a new appreciation for the vital role of Spanish olive oil throughout many centuries. But what was the commodity's connection to the mystical Janus ring? As far as he knew, Robert Arbore never even encountered the key. And as Rosa had asked, was his finding the key behind an empty olive oil carton all those years ago really a tangible connection to Spanish olive oil? Plagued with questions he couldn't answer, his self-doubts rose once again to the surface. Fidgeting in his seat, he thought, *Did I abandon Ann at the worst possible time for a wild goose chase in Almedinilla? Steady yourself,* he repeated to himself again and again as he tightly clenched the armrests on either side of his seat. *I know there is something important to discover in Almedinilla!*

After landing at the Granada International Airport and collecting his luggage, Tony rented a car for the ninety-minute drive north to Almedinilla. Previously, he had emailed Rosa's contact, Pietro Rossi, explaining that he was interested in securing a source of olive oil for his specialty grocery stores and that a mutual colleague, Rosa Martini, had suggested they get together to discuss Tony's needs. The two men had arranged to meet the following day at the Reyes family olive mill where Signore Rossi often worked. Once again, Tony did not want to disclose the true nature of his visit just yet, for fear that Signor Rossi would dismiss him as some kind of lunatic. The Mediterranean diet, with its emphasis on olive oil and other healthy food choices, had become widely popular in America. Therefore, Tony believed that assuming the role of a franchise store owner, who was looking to address the expanding business opportunity presented by America's growing affinity for olive oil, was a perfect ruse.

The beautiful Spanish countryside with its multitude of olive groves dotting the roadway captivated Tony during his drive to the picturesque town of Almedinilla. *Wouldn't this be a fantastic area to explore with Ann?* he momentarily thought to himself before suddenly realizing the dim prospects for such an excursion.

Once in town, he checked into his small hotel, whose architecture reflected the Roman and Moorish influences with its central courtyard gardens, stone floors, mosaic wall tiles, and elaborate, ornamental displays. Tony decided to spend the rest of the day exploring Almedinilla in search of any potential information or clues that could aid him in his mission.

Wandering through the narrow winding streets, with the white facades of its houses and shops silhouetted against the steep mountain ranges and the green glint of its olive groves, Tony felt like he was strolling back in time. *What a beautiful city,* he thought, once again lamenting the fact that he wasn't able to share this experience with Ann. He viewed some of Almedinilla's main tourist attractions, including a well-preserved Roman villa from the first century A.D. and an archeological museum. Although rich in artifacts representing Iberian culture, including the production of olive oil, the museum disappointed Tony for it failed to display any keys that resembled the one he had discovered as a boy. Continuing his tour of the small city, he also failed to detect any trace of a local hospital, health clinic, or research center where a miracle cure might be under development or evaluation. After a quick meal of pescaito frito, or fish fried in, of course, olive oil, at one of the local restaurants, Tony felt the effects of jet lag from his long journey taking hold and returned to his hotel to retire for the night.

The next morning, Tony walked the short distance to the Reyes Family Olive Mill just north of town. He had been instructed to meet Pietro Rossi in the visitors center, where small groups of tourists were already gathering for the popular olive oil tour. He had already texted Signore Rossi that he would be wearing a red cap for identification.

As he entered the center, a well-tanned gentleman of average height, dressed in white slacks and a pale blue polo shirt, approached him and spoke, "With that red cap, you must be Tony Lucas."

Tony nodded assent and offered his hand, responding, "I'm so pleased to meet you."

"I am Pietro Rossi," the man continued as he warmly shook Tony's hand. "It's a pleasure to welcome you to the home of the world's finest olive oil. Please follow me."

Signore Rossi spoke perfect English with a melodic Italian accent. He led Tony past the assembling tourists and into a small private office in the back of the building. Pietro Rossi was an elderly man, perhaps in his mid-seventies, but he had a spry step and a twinkle in his eye that gave him a youthful demeanor. As the two men sat on opposite sides of a small table, Signore Rossi began the conversation. "So, you are interested in sourcing olive oil. Well, you've come to the right place."

During the next several minutes, Tony received a tutorial on the history, virtues, and operations of the Reyes olive oil farm. Signore Rossi explained theirs was a fifth-generation, family-owned operation, who provided unparalleled attention to the production of the finest quality olive oil, or as it was called by the locals, liquid gold. The Reyes owned a modest-sized olive grove of approximately ten hectares in size, where they harvested the popular Picual olive, common to the region and renowned for its high oil yield and exquisite taste. Their mill, or almazara, produced extra virgin olive oil, or EVOO, the highest grade available, via a process that Signore Rossi described in some detail. This entailed first harvesting the olives sometime in the winter months between November and February, depending on the weather. Olives that had fallen to the ground were collected separately and could not be designated EVOO quality. Within twenty-four hours of harvest, the olives must be washed in cold water, ground into a paste, and spun in a centrifuge to extract the high-quality oil. The olive oil was then filtered and decanted for several weeks before bottling in green glass bottles to protect it from harmful ultraviolet rays. Every stage of the operation was strictly controlled, and sampling occurred throughout.

To be considered EVOO, the oil must meet a slew of stringent requirements and achieve a perfect score on an array of quality criteria. No chemicals or additives could touch the oil. It couldn't have any defects in color, smell, or taste as determined by a panel of expert tasters. No heating above 80.6° F during processing was permitted, and it had to have an acidity level lower than 0.8 percent. Pietro Rossi proudly boasted that Reyes olive oil consistently scored lower than 0.3 percent in terms of acid levels.

When SignoreRossi had finished his descriptive narrative, Tony responded with some general questions, professing his ignorance of olive oil and its production. He then asked, "Pietro Rossi sounds like an Italian name. How did you come to work in Spain?"

The elderly gentleman answered, "That is an interesting story, but for now, only the short version. Essentially, I have been in the olive oil business for most of my adult life, first in the Puglia region of Southern Italy, where I was born and raised. There I represented the commercial interests of several local olive mills. Several years ago, many of my clients' groves were infected by a plant bacterium known as Xylella fastidiosa, which eventually killed most of the trees. For this reason, it is called by some the Ebola of olive trees. As my Italian fortunes faded, I was fortunate to discover the wonders of Spanish olive oil, especially the oil from the Reyes mill here in Almedinilla. I started representing their commercial interests and shortly thereafter decided to settle near the mill in the beautiful Andalusian countryside."

After a few more short exchanges, Pietro eyed Tony with a quizzical expression and asked, "Pardon me for asking, but why are you really here?"

Momentarily startled by the penetrating question, Tony repeated the explanation he had provided during their earlier email exchanges. "As I wrote, I own a series of specialty grocery stores back in America and plan to start selling imported olive oil to meet my customers' demands. I came here to investigate potential sources, and Rosa Martini had suggested that we speak."

Pietro gave Tony a sly smile and responded. "Exactly. If you wanted to speak with me, you didn't have to fly three-thousand miles to visit me here in Almedinilla. Also, if you were really interested in sourcing EVOO, I would have expected you to research some information on the subject. Do not take this personally, but you know absolutely nothing about olive oil. So I repeat, why are you really here?"

Tony fidgeted in his chair as he considered his options. Something in Pietro's aged eyes suggested that he would see through any fabrication, so Tony decided to come clean. "I came to Almedinilla to seek a cure for my wife who is dying of ALS, or what is commonly known as Lou Gehrig's disease," he blurted out. "I know it sounds crazy, but I believe that somehow you and Almedinilla may provide clues that can help me."

Pietro looked puzzled and replied, "We know that olive oil has many health benefits and is the staple of the beneficial

Mediterranean diet, but I don't see how Almedinilla oil, or for that matter I, can help your wife."

Tony continued, "May I tell you a story that will hopefully explain why I am here?"

After a momentary pause, Pietro nodded his assent, and Tony spent the next several minutes reviewing the major points of his extraordinary tale, including the ancient Janus key, the futuristic newspaper headlines, the possibility that the letters BMAA-IN suggested the crippling disease of the headline was ALS, the story of Lucius Antonius, the common themes that apparently linked Tony to both Lucius Antonius and Rosa Martini's dad, Robert Arbore, and finally, the clue that led Tony to Almedinilla. Pietro sat attentively through the entire tale, often exhaling an astonished "mamma mia!"

When Tony had finished his story, Pietro rose from his chair and said excitedly, "I must show you something. Can you meet me back here in two hours?"

Wondering what Pietro meant to show him, Tony readily agreed.

CHAPTER TWENTY-FIVE

Tony and Pietro rendezvoused in the same room a few hours later. Expecting Pietro to reveal some object or objects of interest, Tony was a bit surprised that the man carried nothing with him, no bags, boxes, or containers. What could he be up to?

Pietro began speaking. "When you told me your story, I knew I had to show you this." Reaching into his shirt pocket, he pulled out a small bronze key attached to a ring; the key's shaft was sculpted in the shape of an ancient-looking, two-faced man.

Tony was stunned. "That's the key I found as a boy."

"It would appear so. I have often wondered if it had some strange powers, and your story seems to confirm my suspicions."

"How did you find it?" asked Tony, still dumbfounded at the rediscovery of the key that had influenced so many strange events over the last fifty-four years of his life.

"Ah," replied Pietro, "now it's time for my story."

The tale Pietro related to Tony was a fascinating one. Approximately fifty years earlier, on one of his business trips to New York City as a representative of certain Puglia olive mills, he spent a casual afternoon pursuing one of his hobbies, antiquing jewelry pieces. He considered himself a connoisseur of sorts, based on the skills he had cultivated through research, training, and multiple visits to different antique shops across Europe and America. A particular shop in downtown Brooklyn called Brooklyn Treasures, which was noted for its collection of jewelry, books, and other antiques had attracted his attention. Interested in examining its merchandise, he had grabbed the subway from his midtown Manhattan hotel to the Atlantic Avenue station in Brooklyn, near where the shop was located. While perusing the aisles of the quaint store, he happened upon this ancient-looking brass key with the attached ring. From his own experience, this piece struck him as a unique and old artifact, especially with its two-faced icon that he identified as the Roman god Janus. The store's proprietor had no information or authentication papers on the piece but recalled that he had acquired it from a local citizen who had found it on a street in Brooklyn and thought it might be worth something. Pietro purchased the key on the spot.

For the next few years, Pietro carried the ring wherever he went, believing that it was his good luck charm. Indeed, from that time, his business as an olive oil broker expanded into a very lucrative enterprise. That is until the bacterial infection clobbered Puglia with its devastating impact on the olive groves. That was almost thirty years ago, in 1990. During his search for new suppliers, Robert Arbore, who of course was Rosa Martini's father, traveled to meet Pietro in Rome and join him in the search for a new source of olive oil. Up until that time, Robert Arbore's Italian Emporium in Baltimore had been procuring its oil from one of Pietro's client's olive groves in Puglia.

Here the story took a strange twist. On the evening of his arrival in Rome, Robert met Pietro for dinner at a local restaurant to discuss their itinerary and arrange their travel plans. Based on his knowledge of the Italian olive oil industry, Pietro had prepared a portfolio describing six different olive groves throughout Italy for them to visit, focusing on areas that were free of the bacterial infection. He had also included an article from a journal titled *Olive Oil Times* that provided coverage of all things olive oil, including production, recipes, shopping, events, and art. This particular story highlighted the recently completed Lucca Olive Oil Festival, a three-day event that celebrated the end of the harvest for many of the olive farms in the Tuscany area of Italy. At that time, Pietro never even considered Spanish olive groves as a new source; indeed, he knew virtually nothing about Spanish olive oil or its production.

As their discussions continued late into the night, Robert began to surrender to the effects of jet lag from his earlier, transatlantic flight. Ever the courteous host, Pietro suggested that they adjourn for the night and sent Robert back to his hotel with the packet of information for his personal review. Because it was raining heavily that night, Pietro also insisted that Robert carry the portfolio in Pietro's Etruscan leather briefcase, rendered somewhat water-resistant with a coating of waterproof spray. By now, Pietro had grown accustomed to storing his lucky key in the briefcase that he carried with him at virtually all times, and in his haste, had neglected to remove it before handing the briefcase to Robert.

The following afternoon they met again to finalize their itinerary. Before Pietro could utter even a single word, Robert started babbling about an olive grove in Almedinilla, Spain. "It's brilliant!" gushed Robert. "I never even thought of sources outside of Italy. But the olive oil produced by this mill is untouched by any bacterial infection, manufactured to the most exacting standards, and furthermore, is less expensive than any equivalent Italian oil. How can we go wrong? I was so enthusiastic about this source that I took the liberty to call the oil mill this morning and speak with one of the owners, a Senor Alejandro Reyes."

Here Pietro did manage to briefly interrupt Robert, asking him in a wavering tone, "Almedinilla olive oil? How did you get the name and number of the mill?"

Robert looked at him with a puzzled expression as he

answered, "Why, all the information was provided in the magazine article from *Olive Oil Times* that was included in the packet you gave me last night. It described the Almedinilla Olive Oil Festival in great detail. I did wonder about the date of the festival; it was listed as April 15, 1991, next year instead of this year. I suppose that error wasn't picked up by the editors. Anyway, Senor Reyes assured me that he could easily meet our supply requirements and is anxious to host us for a visit to inspect his operations. He even provided me with the specific directions to his mill."

As Pietro was trying to absorb this astonishing information, Robert continued. "By the way, that is some clever little gadget you have in your briefcase. When I pulled out the portfolio this morning, I noticed that old key ring staring at me with the bright red lights from the old man's eyes. It almost seemed as if he was trying to talk to me. How do the lights come on and off? I didn't notice any battery compartment or power source."

Pietro was absolutely dumbfounded. In all the years he had owned this key, it had never illuminated for him, not once. Robert then handed Pietro his briefcase, stating that the key and all the papers in the portfolio were in order.

In response to this new information, all Pietro could manage was a muted agreement with Robert's conclusions about the potential advantages of Spanish olive oil. He simply couldn't think of anything else to say that wouldn't make him sound like a complete idiot. Pietro had never heard of the Reyes Olive Mill in Almedinilla and most certainly didn't include a magazine article describing that city's olive oil festival and dated one year in the future. He had no clue how the story had originated or how it had wound up in his briefcase. His head was spinning with so many unanswered questions. Where in God's name had the information on Almedinilla come from, and was the Reyes Olive Mill even real? How had an article about a festival in Italy been converted to one describing a fiesta in Spain that hadn't even occurred yet? And why did that old key light up for Robert?

Shortly after Robert departed to run some personal errands, Pietro anxiously wrenched the portfolio out of his briefcase to review the listings. He scoured through the packet of papers that included the descriptions of the six Italian mills and the article on the Lucca Olive Festival. Nowhere was there any reference to a future Almedinilla Festival. He also noted the old key, with its Janus icon, darkly staring back at him from the bottom of his briefcase.

During the next several days, Pietro and Robert toured the six Italian olive mills on Pietro's list just as they had agreed to do; however, none of them matched the exact criteria they were seeking, a combination of superior quality, plentiful supply, and competitive pricing. It was then that Robert insisted they fly to Spain and investigate the Reyes Olive Mill in Almedinilla. Pietro had his personal misgivings about such an excursion; after all, the event with the briefcase contents the other night were too strange for him to even broach with Robert. However, business logic eventually prevailed, and he consented to the trip, leaving the travel arrangements to Robert.

The rest of the story was, as Pietro put it, history. Their trip to Almedinilla was a rousing success, and a letter of intent to purchase the Reyes oil was signed. This agreement inaugurated a long and profitable relationship for all parties. Robert returned to America, delighted that he had secured an olive oil source for his Italian emporium, even if it was Spanish oil. Pietro began his tenure as a commercial representative for Reyes olive oil, and as a result, the mill experienced a significant upturn in both visibility and profit. And Pietro became so enamored with the serene Almedinilla countryside that he relocated to the area.

CHAPTER TWENTY-SIX

Pietro paused his storytelling and gave Tony a knowing but furtive smile. "For years, I have thought about that meeting with Robert Arbore. Where did the information on Almedinilla come from, especially the description of its olive oil festival that was still one year away? I suspected the key was somehow involved when Robert told me it was emitting light from Janus's eyes. As I mentioned, it never did so for me. When you told me the key did the same thing for you, I finally knew that my suspicions were correct. Someone must have found the key after it slipped out of your pocket on that Brooklyn street, and it wound up at the antique store where I first noticed it. As soon as it encountered Robert Arbore, it revealed the Reyes Olive Mill in the town of Almedinilla to him."

Tony was trying to process all this new information from Pietro's amazing narrative. Thinking out loud, he blurted, "Your story about Robert Arbore parallels mine and Lucius's in so many ways. An ancient key mysteriously illuminates as it reveals new information that predicts future outcomes. And as far as we know, this new information was visible only to the three of us, who apparently have some special aptitude for time. I'm convinced more than ever that the key was sending important messages to assist us with our specific problems. Those messages helped rescue Lucius Antonius's olive oil trade, and replenish Robert Arbore's principal commercial asset, also olive oil. I believe my message is intended to save my wife and that somehow olive oil is involved in the cure. And if the key led both Robert and me to Almedinilla, it must be where I'm supposed to find the answer."

"Perhaps you are correct in your assessment," answered Pietro, "but if all three of you are somehow linked by this key, how does Almedinilla tie in with the Roman merchant? I didn't hear you speak of any connection between Lucius Antonius and Almedinilla."

"That doesn't mean there wasn't one," answered Tony. "We know that Lucius secured his olive oil from southern Spain; it could very well have been in the area we now know as Almedinilla."

Pietro nodded in agreement and spoke. "With your wife's condition, I fully appreciate your urgency in exploring Almedinilla. Let me offer you my services in any way that I may help. And as a start, please accept this." He then unfolded his right hand, exposing the key, and handed it to Tony. "It never spoke to me, but obviously, it did so to you. You were meant to have it. May it aid you in your search."

Tony was moved by this generous gesture, and after taking a moment to gather his emotions, thanked Pietro for his kindness. Holding the key in his hand, he somehow felt that he had come full circle, tying his past from fifty-four years ago as an eighth-grade schoolboy in St. Bridget's to his present situation here in Almedinilla.

CHAPTER TWENTY-SEVEN

Tony's rediscovery of the ancient key reinvigorated his passion to unravel the mystery of the miracle cure from the newspaper headline. Deep in his heart, he felt he was on the right track; there were just too many strange and unpredictable connections with all the players who had experienced the time-bending power of the ancient key. And if the key had helped Lucius Antonius and Robert Arbore solve their problems, why wouldn't it help Tony with his? He mapped out a strategy for his mission. Taking advantage of Pietro's generous offer to help, Tony asked him to reach out to as many of his neighbors and co-workers as possible and inquire if any of them had any knowledge of a potential olive-based cure for ALS under development. If Tony's hunch was correct, Almedinilla olive trees were a crucial element in such a cure. Tony also requested that Pietro ask people about George Janusowski. He told Pietro, "The newspaper article of 2025 indicates that this individual is an important player in this mystery. Locating him may provide the pathway to a cure."

For his part, Tony initiated a systematic campaign to identify and contact clinics and research centers in the Cordoba area where new medicines based on olive oil research might be discovered and/or tested. Using his Almedinilla hotel room as a home base, he engaged in phone conversations with as many scientists and representatives from these institutes as possible.

The cordiality and cooperation of the Spanish populace amazed him. Virtually everyone he called spoke perfectly comprehensible English, and after a brief explanation that he was seeking information to potentially aid his sick wife, most of them readily agreed to answer his questions. Tony vowed that no matter how things turned out, he would never forget the many acts of kindness displayed toward him by the local citizenry.

Tony discovered that the two major biomedical research centers in the province of Cordoba were the University of Cordoba and the Maimonides Biomedical Research Institute. Unfortunately, no one he spoke with from either institution had any information on promising new treatments for ALS or any other brain disorder. He then expanded his search area beyond Cordoba to institutes in other provinces of the olive-rich Andalusian area, including the University of Granada and the University of Seville. Again, nothing relevant to his search emerged from talks with representatives from either center. His spirits briefly rose when he learned of the Center for Advanced Studies of Olive Groves and Olive Oil at the University of Jaen. This facility was a prominent international hub for innovation in the olive oil sector. Based on the name alone, Tony reasoned it would be a likely source of any medical breakthroughs based on olive products. However, once again, no information that could aid Ann emerged from this lead. Tony's frustration grew even more pronounced when Pietro reported similar negative results from his multiple conversations with various residents of Almedinilla.

During his time in Spain, Tony stayed in constant communication with his family back home via phone and email. The news was not good. He learned that Ann was regressing rapidly, and her palliative team had already recommended breathing support via noninvasive ventilation, which meant breathing through a face mask connected via tubes to a small portable ventilator. While this was generally an innocuous treatment, Tony knew that in ALS patients, it often preceded the more radical intervention of invasive mechanical ventilation. In that procedure, a tracheostomy is performed, during which a plastic tube is inserted through an opening in the neck into the windpipe or trachea, and an external ventilator machine takes over the respiratory work. When Ann reached this stage, her condition would be dire.

In other disturbing news, Tony learned that Ann's companion cat Holly had suddenly died. This was a terrible shock; both he and Ann loved their pet. In recent months, she had been one of the few sources of comfort to Ann, often nestling into a rounded ball of soft fur, contentedly purring on Ann's lap. Tony couldn't help but wonder if this was some harbinger of future tragedy.

Tony wanted to return home as soon as possible but knew his work here in Almedinilla was not completed. Yes, he had reclaimed the mysterious key, but that alone was not enough. There were several more institutes in Spain to contact and many more people to speak with. With just one more piece of tangible information, he believed the whole puzzle could fit together. However, it was the disturbing news about Ann's decline that eventually swayed his decision. Tony couldn't fathom his despair if he was three thousand miles away while Ann lay dying. He knew he had to return home to his wife. Fortunately, he was able to book a return flight back to Philadelphia via Madrid for the following day.

The next morning, Tony and Pietro met for a farewell breakfast meeting. Pietro reiterated his wonder at the tantalizing tale of the Janus key and pledged to continue seeking information on a possible cure for ALS from the Almedinilla community. For his part, Tony could barely express his gratitude for everything

Pietro had done, including, of course, gifting the key.

"Do not think about it for a moment," retorted Pietro, "As I said, you were meant to have it. I fervently hope it will lead you to the cure you seek." With that, the two men embraced, and Tony strode to his car for the drive back to the Granada International Airport.

CHAPTER TWENTY-EIGHT

If Tony managed to sleep at all during the seven-hour transit over the Atlantic Ocean, he surely couldn't remember when. Even as the powerful jet turbines provided a monotonous background hum, his brain churned with unrelenting anxiety over Ann's deteriorating condition and his inability to find any answers for her. Scanning the vast expanse of the Atlantic thirty-eight thousand feet below him, he wondered how many miles remained on his interminable flight. His Almedinilla visit had failed to uncover a cure or even a single, concrete clue that might provide a path to a remedy. Yes, he had reclaimed the key, courtesy of Pietro Rossi, but in reality, the cold analytical facts did not lie. He was coming home empty-handed, at least in terms of any uplifting news for Ann.

A fitting end to his gloomy flight greeted him at the Philadelphia International Airport as he joined the masses in what seemed like an endless queue to clear customs. By the time Tony was finally freed to claim his luggage, he was mentally and physically exhausted.

Andrew was waiting curbside to pick up his father as he exited the baggage claim area. Tony's first words were, "How is your mother doing?"

"She's slipping fast; I'm glad you're home. She needs you

now more than ever."

Tony experienced a fresh pang of guilt at his absence over the past several days but quickly suppressed his feelings as he listened to Andrew's sobering update during the drive home. Tony then reported that his own mission, purportedly to confer with a physician who championed a novel, holistic approach to prolong the life of ALS patients, was virtually useless. Lying to his son bothered Tony; he swore to himself that he would soon reveal the truth about the key to his children.

Despite Andrew's warning about his mother's dismal condition, Tony was unprepared for the shocking apparition that greeted him at home. Hunched over in a wheelchair, Ann could barely lift her head. Her body was cadaverously thin, a mere shell of her former athletic physique. With her every breath, a life and death struggle seemed to ensue, as reflected by the labored wheezing sounds emitted with each intake. An unused ventilator mask and a portable respirator unit were lying on the floor next to her chair. As she slowly raised her head in an effort to speak, Tony observed excessive drool streaming from her mouth.

He rushed to his wife and embraced her in a tender hug. "I will never leave you again," he muttered quietly to her.

Signaling for Ann to resist the urge to speak, Tony quickly summarized his story from Almedinilla. Following his short narrative, he grimly concluded, "I found the key but nothing more. There was no cure in Almedinilla." He then pulled the key out of his pocket and displayed it to Ann, whose eyes glistened as she stared at the ancient artifact.

She gently squeezed his hand and quietly uttered, "What will be, will be; you've done everything you could."

As Ann was resting, Tony contemplated her last words to him. Have I done everything I could? he thought to himself. In his mind, he retraced the series of events over the past several weeks, recognizing that, like falling dominoes, each individual event had triggered a subsequent chapter in his quest for a cure. His meeting with Ethel Warburg at the Met had led him to Professor Saxon and the revelation about Lucius Antonius. In turn, this story had prompted him to ponder the cryptic slogans on Rosa Martini's delivery truck and subsequently to speak with her. From this discussion, he had gleaned information about Robert Arbore's connection to Almedinilla, which spurred him to travel to Spain, where he met Pietro Rossi and reclaimed the ancient key. In retrospect, it truly was a remarkable saga with so many surprising twists and turns. But now, were there any more acts to play out, or was it game over with the return of the key after a fifty-four-year hiatus? Unless Pietro managed to uncover some relevant information, there was no new lead to explore.

Furthermore, Tony knew that Ann's condition was critical, and any remaining time to help her was quickly eroding. Perhaps it was too late already. Desolately, he stared at the lifeless and dark Janus key and lamented their situation.

Life turned even more dismal in the next few days as Tony, Ann, and their children started to address some end-of-life decisions with her palliative team. Ann was adamant about two primary concerns, and she made Tony promise to abide by them. First, she didn't want to be a burden to her family; secondly, she wanted to spend her remaining days at home rather than in the sterile environment of some hospital or nursing home. She was also worried about potential cognitive decline, a problem common to many late-stage ALS patients.

They had already formulated a living will that named Tony as her healthcare agent, and at Ann's insistence, they spent some time reviewing its provisions. Should she reach the stage where she could not make decisions for herself, Ann had given specific directions that she did not want invasive mechanical ventilation or cardiopulmonary resuscitation used to prolong her life.

Tony felt like a messenger of doom as he began to inform

close family and friends that the end was approaching. In spite of her weakened immune system and the enhanced risk of developing pneumonia, he was reluctant to deny anyone a last opportunity to visit Ann and bid their goodbyes, knowing the wonderful impact she had had on so many peoples' lives over the years. His decision resulted in a steady stream of daily callers and visitors, including close friends, teaching colleagues, and even former students, all anxious to check in on Ann and to console Tony. However, it was heartbreaking to witness Ann's efforts at communicating with her visitors and family. Her near loss of speech represented perhaps the biggest psychological impact of this dreadful disease. During several encounters, she actually experienced periods of intense sobbing out of frustration in trying to verbalize her thoughts into words. Nevertheless, Tony knew that Ann was moved by the many emotional encounters with different sympathizers.

One unexpected visitor was Dr. Smith, Ann's primary caretaker, who had been kind enough to stop by and monitor her condition. Tony recalled how, as a young kid in Brooklyn, he and his sister would often accompany their pediatrician father on drives to his many house calls. Back then, visiting sick patients in their homes was just a routine part of being a physician. Now house calls were so rare that they were regarded as special events, sort of like an exceptional service way above and beyond the norm. His boyhood remembrances didn't in any way diminish his gratitude to Dr. Smith for the personal house call, but it did cause him to reflect on how things had changed over the years. As expected, Dr. Smith's visit offered no new hope for Ann; her situation was grave, and without mechanical intervention, she would soon succumb to respiratory failure.

In terms of spiritual guidance, both Ann and Tony found some peace and comfort in the visits of their parish pastor, Father Simmons of St. John's Church, and his universal message that death is an essential part of the Catholic faith. Ann had discussed with him her desire to avoid invasive mechanical ventilation and to allow the disease to progress on its natural course. His response was enlightening to both of them. They learned that the Church does not promote vitalism, the preservation of physical life at all costs, but rather emphasizes the qualities of individual dignity and compassion in the last days of life. The Church also taught that it was permissible to refuse medical treatment if, in the patient's judgment, those means offered no reasonable hope of benefit or if they placed an excessive burden or expense on the family.

Concerning their finances, Tony had never hesitated, even for an instant, to weigh the economic costs of his obsessive efforts to find a potential cure; saving Ann was all that mattered. But now, with the end rapidly approaching, he had to admit that the various trips, including his Spanish escapade, coupled with the skyrocketing outlays for Ann's palliative care, were draining their savings at an alarming rate. Still, no concern, especially a financial one, could even begin to approach the depths of the unimaginable sadness at the prospect of losing his beloved wife and the unmitigated disappointment at his failure to find a cure for her terrible disease. Tony felt as if he had hit rock bottom.

CHAPTER TWENTY-NINE

Tony stared morosely at the ancient key in his hand. He had adopted the habit of carrying it with him at all times and examining it countless times during the day for any hint of a sparkle or glimmer of light. His excitement at rediscovering it in Almedinilla initially triggered hope that, somehow, it would again work its extraordinary magic and reveal the cure he was seeking. However, this aspiration had all but vanished as the Janus image remained dark and lifeless, day after day. His impassioned efforts over the past several weeks had been based on the assumption that the crippling disease in the newspaper story from his youth was ALS. In reality, though, that assumption was just that, a conjecture with no unequivocal proof behind it. Perhaps his association of BMAA in the article to ALS was no more than wishful thinking, and his recent missions were, in fact, nothing but a fool's errand. *Oh well,* he thought to himself, *at this point, it really doesn't matter.*

The piercing ringing of the landline phone stirred Tony out of his doldrums. His first impulse was to ignore it; so many people had phoned in recent days that he was growing weary of repeating the same depressing news about Ann's condition. However, some unknown impulse impelled him to walk to the other side of the room and glance at the receiver. His reaction was one of mild surprise at the LCD display flashing International. Who would be calling from overseas? As he picked up the receiver and uttered, "Hello," he recognized the sharply accented tone of Pietro Rossi.

"Tony!" he explained, "I found something."

Tony immediately came out of his stupor as a surge of adrenaline pulsed through his system in response to these hopeful words.

"I just finished speaking with a young lady who works in the Reyes olive groves. She told me that her fiancé works as Vice President of Business Development for a small, Polish pharmaceutical company that has been exploring bioactive compounds extracted from the Picual olive tree. They even have a compound ready to start testing in clinical trials as an anti-inflammatory agent for the treatment of arthritis."

Tony's hopes faded as he digested these words from Pietro, and he interjected in a disappointed tone, "That's interesting news, but I don't see how that helps us at all; arthritis is not ALS."

"I know, but here's the real news. Her fiancé's name is George Janusowski."

Tony felt the blood drain from his face and his eyes well up in tears as he struggled to absorb this staggering information. After all these years, the unknown man in the newspaper article had been discovered. Could this person actually be Ann's savior, even at this late-stage, eleventh-hour of her crisis? Responding to Pietro in a shaky and halting voice, he heard himself mutter, "George Janusowski?"

"That's right, and get this. His fiancé tells me he is in the United States right now, visiting different investor groups to seek funding for his company's clinical program. This week he is in New York City attending an investor conference. You have to try and connect with him up there. This is the opportunity you've been waiting for."

Tony spent the next few minutes speaking with Pietro, learning more details about his amazing discovery. Pietro related how he had continued his search for information on a potential cure for ALS after Tony's departure from Almedinilla. Following scores of fruitless conversations with several of his colleagues and neighbors, he had just about reached his wit's end when he stumbled upon a young woman named Dolores Vidal in, of all places, a cheese shop in Almedinilla. Pietro took notice of the woman standing in line because she was carrying a tote bag with a University of Barcelona logo. Knowing that the college was a leading research center in Spain, he struck up a conversation with her. To his surprise, he discovered that Dolores, a student at the university, spent much of the olive harvest season that ran from November to February helping her family in their traditional business of olive picking in the Reyes groves. When Pietro pressed her about potential medicinal uses of olive oil, she readily offered information about her fiancé and his role at Pol Pharma, a Polish pharmaceutical company based in Warsaw. She explained that the company focused on drug discovery for inflammatory diseases such as osteoarthritis, the common joint disorder affecting millions of sufferers. The two had met at the university where he was visiting with several prominent faculty members to discuss potential sources and applications of bioactive compounds derived from olive trees, and she was working as a research assistant for one of the professors. Dolores eventually directed him to Almedinilla, where he secured a supply of Picaul olive leaves from the Reyes grove for his company's research. From that point, matters advanced quickly on both a personal and professional level. Their relationship developed into a strong and loving bond that led to their engagement. Meanwhile, his company's chemists synthesized a potential clinical compound for osteoarthritis from a precursor molecule that was derived from the olive leaf extracts.

Intrigued by her story, Pietro had asked for the name of her fiancé and discovered it was George Janusowski. Recovering from his momentary shock at this startling disclosure, Pietro mentioned he had a colleague in the United States who would be anxious to speak with George. That's when Dolores revealed George's visit to New York. As Vice President of Business Development, one of his principal responsibilities was to secure funding sources required for the expensive clinical evaluation of their compound. J.P. Morgan Chase, the large banking and investment firm, periodically hosted information symposia to introduce potential investors to small, relatively unknown life science companies seeking funding. Pol Pharma had been invited to the latest conference, and George was scheduled to present on behalf of the company at the New York symposium in two days.

After all this time and effort, Tony still couldn't quite believe that George Janusowski was identified. Profoundly moved by Pietro's assistance, Tony thanked him profusely. "I just can't express what your discovery means for us. I'm forever in your debt, and I hope I can repay you in some way down the road."

Pietro graciously acknowledged Tony's thanks and replied, "My payment will be seeing the prophecy from the key fulfilled, and your wife recovered from her disease." Tony enthusiastically agreed to apprise Pietro of all future developments with George Janusowski.

Tony grabbed his computer and immediately Googled the J.P. Morgan Global Life Sciences Symposium. He learned that the conference, scheduled at the Marquis Marriott Hotel in mid-Manhattan, was designed to facilitate interactions between emerging life science company representatives and top-tier investors through presentations, panel discussions, and one-on-one meetings. He also realized that attendance was by invitation only. Thinking rapidly, he called his sister Karen, who was a Vice

President at J. P. Morgan's Consumer and Community Banking Division based in Jacksonville, Florida.

Upon answering the phone, Karen's first words, spoken in an alarmed tone, were, "Is this about Ann?" From her recent visit, Karen knew that the situation was dire and was bracing herself for some terrible news.

"Yes, it is," replied Tony, "But it's not what you think." He then proceeded to explain that he was interested in attending the J. P. Morgan's Global Life Science Symposium later that week in New York to meet with a company that was seeking investment for its novel ALS program. He wasn't ready to explain the true details to his sister.

"Tony," replied Karen. "Do you think it's really wise to leave Ann at this stage? And will some early research on ALS offer any real hope for her?"

"Trust me, this is really important, and I'm only planning to be in New York for a couple of hours on Thursday. But I need an invitation to attend the conference."

Karen agreed to investigate and promised to get back to him within the hour. Thirty minutes later, she called with the news that she had wrangled an invitation for Tony from one of her colleagues in the Investment Division and that the required documentation would be emailed to him later that afternoon. Tony thanked her and promised to keep her updated on both his trip and Ann's condition.

Tony next turned to the matter of informing Ann. Realistically, he knew that meeting with George Janusowski was his last hope for her; acute respiratory failure could develop any day, and that would spell the end. He also recognized that this whole exercise was a long shot at best. Expecting a last-minute miracle was unabashed, wishful thinking. But he was certain of one thing; he had to try!

He decided that, as usual, the best approach with Ann was

the direct one. He approached her reclining form on the hospital bed in the family room, again noting the labored, sporadic breathing. If anything, she looked even paler and thinner than just a few hours ago when they last spoke. Looking down at her dull, lethargic eyes, he began, "Ann dear, I have some remarkable news. Pietro Rossi discovered George Janusowski, the man mentioned in the newspaper article that I read about fifty-four years ago. He works for a small pharmaceutical company in Poland and is visiting New York this week to meet with potential investors. I have to go to New York on Thursday for a few hours to meet him and try to uncover the mystery of the message from the key. If anyone has information on a cure, it has to be him. This could be our salvation."

Ann returned his gaze listlessly. Tony wondered if his words had even registered with her. However, his heart jumped as he felt a slight squeeze on his hand and heard her nearly inaudible voice utter, "Go."

When Monica and Andrew stopped by the house later that afternoon for their daily visit, Tony updated them on his plans to attend the New York life sciences investors forum on Thursday.

"Really, Dad," answered Monica, "none of your trips over the past several weeks, including Spain, have led to anything, and now with Mom on her deathbed, you're leaving her again. I just don't get it." Andrew nodded in agreement with his sister's assertion.

Tony understood their renewed frustration with him. From their perspective, it appeared as if he were denying reality by chasing fleeting dreams. He again promised himself he would tell them everything, but with the investor conference and a possible meeting with George Janusowski looming on the horizon, now was not the time. Instead, he pulled out the ancient key ring from his pocket, and for the first time, displayed it to his children. "Trust me," he said. "There is some kind of mysterious messaging associated with this key. I first found it over fifty years ago, and I rediscovered it in Spain during my recent trip. It forecast certain events to me as a kid, and now it may hold the secret to Mom's recovery. I know it sounds crazy, but I promise to tell you everything in a few days. Now I have to get ready for New York."

Both children looked at him with startled expressions but checked their urge to question him. They had completely trusted their father for their entire lives, and they owed him their continued loyalty even in these disconcerting times.

CHAPTER THIRTY

On Thursday morning, Tony boarded the six o'clock Amtrak train at the Wilmington train station bound for New York's Penn Station. Arriving in Manhattan approximately ninety minutes later, he exited the subterranean station and joined the masses of pedestrians jockeying for position on the city sidewalks. The weather was grey and bleak, with a cold April breeze blowing in from the east. *So much for a bright spring day*, he thought to himself, hoping the dreary weather did not portend a dismal outcome. As he walked the twelve blocks north towards the Marriott Marquis on Forty-sixth Street, he recalled his earlier visit with Ethel Warburg at the Metropolitan Museum of Art. Was it only a few weeks ago? That trip now seemed like a distant memory.

Tony entered the hotel through its Broadway entrance and strolled into its famous atrium lobby, soaring forty-eight stories in the air above him. In preparing for this meeting, Tony learned that the hotel was the second largest in the city, with nearly two thousand guest rooms and suites. The Marriott was the first major project in the Times Square revitalization program of the 1980s and is credited with helping transform that area from a seedy, sex-shop filled zone into a family-friendly tourist stop.

The conference was scheduled to begin at eight-fifteen, and Tony arrived early in hopes of cornering George Janusowski ahead of his presentation. Upon registering at the front desk outside the large Broadway Ballroom, the venue for the conference, he was given a badge labeled Anthony Marcus; Status-Guest and a small tote bag emblazoned with the words, J.P. Morgan Global Life Science Investor Conference. Inside the bag was a sheaf of papers, including a program containing background information on each presenting company, an agenda for the two-day symposium, and a courtesy copy of the daily New York Times. He immediately turned the program book to the Pol Pharma page, where a picture of George Janusowski, Vice President of Business Development, was displayed. Armed with this information, he roamed the halls, clustered with small groups of mingling registrants, searching in vain for George.

Twenty minutes later, dispirited at not locating him, he answered the loud ringing chime signaling the start of the conference by joining his fellow attendees as they shuffled into the main ballroom. Tony took an aisle seat near the back door so he could monitor entries by late attendees and listened as the moderator, a nerdy-looking, rail-thin young man who seemed as if he belonged in high school but probably had graduated from one of the top-tier business schools in the country, introduced the symposium. He explained that company presentations were slated for fifteen minutes, with a five-minute question and answer session following each talk. From the agenda, Tony noted that George Janusowski's presentation was the fourth one of the morning sessions, scheduled for ten-ten.

After the first two speakers had completed their lectures, Tony's anxiety about George Janusowski's continued absence grew more intense. How ironic would it be if, after all this effort, George failed to appear? However, midway through the third speaker's presentation describing a novel antisense drug for pancreatic cancer, Tony observed a tall man enter the darkened conference room. As he strolled quietly down the aisle towards the front of the room, Tony could just discern the profile of George Janusowski. He breathed a sigh of relief; at least he was there!

A few minutes later, Tony perked up in his chair and listened attentively as the moderator introduced George Janusowski from Pol Pharma in Poland. Tony didn't want to miss a single word of the presentation in case there was a mention, or even a hint, of a potential treatment for ALS.

George spoke perfect English with a slight Polish accent; perhaps he had been schooled in Britain or the United States. He introduced his talk by describing Pol Pharma's mission statement: "To alleviate the suffering of millions of arthritis sufferers by providing effective and safe products derived from natural source precursors." After reviewing the corporate structure of his company, he proceeded to describe the history and properties of their lead compound, designated Pol-1905. *That's strange,* thought Tony. *Those are the same numbers as the year of the original newspaper from the St. Bridget's time capsule.* Nineteen and five are also the combination of my old safe where I stored my notes from that newspaper. *Is all that merely a coincidence or a possible signal that I'm on the right path?*

As George continued his presentation, Tony learned that leaves derived from the pruning of olive trees represent a valuable source of bioactive compounds. Over the years, many investigative studies had demonstrated the important biological properties of such molecules, including anti-proliferative, anti-atherosclerotic, and cardioprotective effects. As a result, olive leaf extracts were sold across the globe as food supplements with documented health benefits. With this background information, Pol Pharma had initiated a program to identify compounds from olive leaf extracts as starting materials for synthesizing novel molecules with potential anti-inflammatory properties. Company chemists first isolated a phenol-containing compound from the leaf extracts of the Picual olive tree that was amenable to chemical modification. Then, using various chemical reactions that seemed like Greek to Tony, George described how different molecules were synthesized and tested for activity in an in vitro anti-inflammatory assay, which is a test performed in a test tube or in a plastic well rather than in an animal or human subject. This assay involved stimulating whole blood with a molecule called LPS and measuring the production of various inflammatory molecules called cytokines. George referred to the whole process as determining structural-activity relationships for the various test compounds.

From the different molecules that had been assayed, one stood out for its potent activity in blocking cytokine production; it was designated Pol-1905. Subsequently, this compound was tested in vivo models of arthritis using live mice and found to be very effective. George did not display the structure of Pol-1905 for fear that competitor companies would copy it and claim it as their own. Rather, the company had filed a series of patents to protect their proprietary molecule.

In light of the promising profile of Pol-1905, Pol Pharma was anxious to secure funding to advance it into human clinical trials as a potential treatment for osteoarthritis; that's what had brought George to New York. The millions of patients who suffer from this joint disease make it a very lucrative market for pharmaceutical firms. Pol Pharma was seeking a $20-million investment to support the first two phases of clinical testing; Phase I, during which a compound is tested for safety in small numbers of normal volunteers, and Phase II, when different doses of the compound are evaluated in larger numbers of patients to determine if it has any biological effect. In addition to financing these human trials, funds would also be allocated to support additional studies required by the Food and Drug Administration or FDA. This included toxicity, to evaluate the compound's safety in two different animal species; ADME, an acronym for absorption, distribution, metabolism, and excretion, to determine the disposition of the compound in test animals; manufacturing, to assure that the company could synthesize the compound safely according to GMP or good manufacturing practices; and stability, to ascertain that the compound did not disintegrate under defined storage conditions. All this work would be required before the pivotal and expensive Phase III studies could commence, in which a drug's true benefit is examined through lengthy and large clinical trials, often involving thousands of patients and costing hundreds of millions of dollars. And even that enormous expenditure does not guarantee success—that is, FDA approval for the drug.

Wow, thought Tony to himself. *Drug development is certainly complicated and lengthy. No wonder there are so few large pharmaceutical firms. How many companies could afford that type of expense and risk?*

George concluded his presentation by thanking the audience for their attention and reminding them he would be pleased to address any questions now or after the sessions were completed.

As George was answering a few general questions from different attendees, Tony pondered what he had heard, or more specifically, what he had not heard. Not a mention was made throughout the presentation of ALS, or for that matter, any disease of the central nervous system. That probably explained, at least in part, why George Janusowski had not been identified in Tony's earlier Internet searches. He had been utilizing search terms relating to ALS and brain diseases, not arthritis, a disease of the joints. Frustratingly, the essential question with Pol-1905 remained unanswered; could it represent a treatment for Ann?

To his scientifically unsophisticated mind, Tony couldn't even begin to decipher how Pol-1905 might influence ALS;

perhaps it didn't. However, just at that moment, an answer to a question from an audience member offered him a small glimmer of hope. In response to a query about the mechanism of action of Pol-1905, George replied that Pol Pharma scientists were still investigating this matter. However, in preliminary studies, they had observed that the compound stimulated the formation of new chondrocytes, cells in the joints that produce the cartilage matrix. Until recently, it was believed that adult chondrocytes resist proliferation or increasing their numbers through cell division. This accounted for the limited ability of adult cartilage to repair itself after injury. Tony remembered that neurons or nerve cells in the brain also resisted proliferation, explaining the difficulty of recovering from severe brain injuries or disorders. *If Pol-1905 stimulated the development of new chondrocytes, perhaps it was also capable of stimulating neurogenesis, that is, new neuron development in the brain.* At this juncture, Tony had little choice but to believe that Pol-1905 was the miracle cure referred to in that newspaper story from his youth.

CHAPTER THIRTY-ONE

As a bell chimed, signaling the end of Pol Pharma's question and answer period, George strolled off the stage and seated himself in the front row. He stayed seated for the duration of the remaining morning sessions, at which point the moderator announced that lunch would be served in the adjacent room. Tony observed George joining the mass exodus of people flooding out of the conference room and quickly maneuvered to take a position directly behind him. He gently tapped the young man on the shoulder, and as George turned to face him, Tony extended his right hand and spoke. "I really enjoyed your presentation. My name is Tony Lucas. May I join you for lunch?"

George took the proffered hand, uttered a quick thanks, and said he had already made plans to lunch with representatives from Pfizer, one of the world's largest pharmaceutical companies, but he was sure there would be room at the table for him.

Tony trailed George into the dining area where circular tables, each with eight chairs, were set up for the meal. He noticed a group of four people already seated, two men and two women, who were beckoning to George to join them. George made his way to an empty chair in the middle of the group, and Tony, somewhat sheepishly, seated himself in a chair on the opposite side of the table. This must be the Pfizer group, he thought to himself. As George was introducing himself to his fellow diners, Tony studied him carefully. He was tall, just a bit shorter than Tony, at about six feet, and stocky. He looked to be about thirty years old, with pale skin and black hair parted down the middle. He reminded Tony of a young Mike Meyers, the famous comedian from *Saturday Night Live*. Meanwhile, two other conference attendees filled the empty seats on either side of Tony.

As waiters started to serve a first-course salad, one of the late arrivals turned to Tony and introduced himself as John Shillings from the investment firm of Merrill Lynch. Handing Tony a business card, he asked, "Where are you from?"

From his meeting with Jim Cahill at the local chapter of the ALS Association several months earlier, Tony had learned that the exchange of business cards was a ritual practiced by attendees at scientific conferences. He even had some cards hastily printed for this meeting, listing his name, contact information, and a title of Technical Writer clearly inscribed in dark black letters. Tony didn't want to pose as an investor; his ignorance on the subject would probably expose him as a phony should any serious discussions ensue. Instead, he identified himself to John Shillings as a journalist covering the conference for the Delaware Biotech Association based in Wilmington, Delaware.

Unfortunately, John turned out to be a loquacious companion, and he droned on throughout most of the meal about the importance of external funding sources to drive the discovery of the next generation of innovative therapies for unmet clinical needs. Trying not to be overly rude, Tony constantly tuned him out in an effort to decipher the conversations between George and the Pfizer folks on the other side of the table. Unfortunately, the distance between their chairs, coupled with the loud background noise emanating from over one-hundred and fifty people eating and speaking in the same room, rendered most of the conversation inaudible to Tony's ears. However, he did pick up certain phrases, including, "This fits very well with the Pfizer portfolio," "We have a rich history of funding small pharma partners," "The molecule has interesting properties," and "Will you be joining us tonight?" From these tidbits, Tony deduced that the Pfizer reps, who were doing most of the talking, were trying to persuade George to consider their company as the partner of choice for Pol Pharma.

Frustrated, as the lunch session was nearing its end and the dessert course of lemon cake was being served, Tony excused himself in the middle of John Shilling's latest discourse, rose from his chair, and walked around the table to face George directly. "Excuse me," he said, interrupting one of the Pfizer reps in mid-sentence. "It's very important that we talk. I have a proposition that you will find truly amazing. Can we meet in private somewhere?"

The astounded expressions on everyone's faces signaled to Tony that he had committed a serious breach of protocol by interrupting ongoing business discussions between potential partners. However, at this point, he didn't care; time was running out, and he had to speak with George. Tony continued, "I'm sorry to interrupt here, but I really must speak with you. I guarantee you will not regret it."

Displaying an annoyed expression, George replied in a stern tone, "Normally, I don't respond well to interruptions, especially one so rude as this. My schedule is full for the rest of the day, and I am leaving New York tomorrow. If you need to speak with me, leave me your business card, and I will try to reach you when I return home."

Clearly, George had no intention of speaking with Tony; he was extremely upset at the disruption caused by this ill-mannered stranger. The whole affair was going south quickly. Desperate to secure a meeting with this man who represented the last possible chance for Ann, he played his trump card. "I know your fiancée, Dolores Vidal; she assured me you would meet with me here in New York."

"You know Dolores?"

"Yes, we met in Almedinilla during my recent trip there," lied Tony. "She was the one who recommended that we speak."

At the mention of Dolores, George's expression had visibly lightened, and he even managed a sly smile. "Well, if Dolores says so, then it is okay with me. I will have a few minutes at two this afternoon. I'll meet you back here then."

Thanking George and apologizing to the Pfizer people for the interruption, Tony walked back to his seat.

After a few more minutes, Tony remained sitting in the dining room as the other attendees poured out to resume the afternoon sessions in the adjoining conference room. Against the clatter of clanging china and ringing glasses made by servers clearing the tables, Tony debated his strategy for the meeting with George. He knew he had to be forceful in appealing to George's better judgment but not appear as a crazed lunatic spouting unbelievable stories and hypotheses. Unfortunately, he was already at a disadvantage in trying to earn George's trust due to his lie about meeting Dolores. But that fabrication had proven necessary; otherwise, the meeting wouldn't be happening.

By the time the large overhead clock chimed two o'clock, Tony was alone with his thoughts in the cavernous room. He then noticed George approaching in a hurried cadence. George sat down, and they silently slid their respective business card towards one another.

In a curt tone, George began, "I only have a few minutes before my next meeting, so let's get right down to business. What's so important that you had to meet with me?"

His brusque style surprised Tony; no introductions or pleasantries. Apparently, he was still miffed at Tony's rude behavior during lunch. Tony countered, "What if I told you that your compound, Pol-1905, represented a miracle cure for a crippling brain disease that affects thousands of patients across the globe with paralyzing symptoms and premature death?"

George frowned as he answered, "I would say you must know something that none of our scientists do. And since you have no connection whatsoever with Pol Pharma, at least as far as I know, I would tend to doubt your assertion."

"But that's exactly it; I do know something that no one else knows. And I can prove it to you. Provide me a small sample of Pol-1905, and I'll show you."

Tony knew he had gone way out on a limb with his request for a sample, but George's subsequent harsh response still stung.

"This is utter nonsense. You entice me here and then expect me to turn over a sample of our proprietary compound? Why? So, you can decipher its structure and use that information to make additional molecules or invalidate our Pol-1905 patent claims? You must take me for a fool. I assure you that is not going to happen." With those words, George started to rise from his seat to leave.

"Please wait," pleaded Tony. "I mean no harm to you or your company. It's just that my wife of nearly forty years is dying from ALS, and I believe your compound can save her life. We are literally at the end of our options as she only has days, or maybe hours, to live."

George sat back in his chair and spoke in a somewhat softer tone. "Look, I'm terribly sorry about your wife, but there are a hundred reasons why I can't give you a sample of Pol-1905. My company would have to execute an MTA—a Material Transfer Agreement—with you, specifying exactly how you plan to use the compound. And giving it your wife is totally out of the question; at this stage, it is only an experimental compound, and no studies with humans are permitted. In addition, there isn't a shred of evidence that Pol-1905 has any efficacy in diseases other than arthritis, let alone ALS. And beyond those reasons, while I do have a small supply of Pol-1905 with me, that entire amount is already earmarked for another company that has signed an MTA with us. I would be breaking too many company regulations to count if I were to furnish any of the compound to you."

As George finished speaking, Tony pulled out the ancient key from his jacket pocket. "This key doesn't care about all those reasons; I found it as a boy, and it has predicted certain events before they actually occurred. It has also predicted that your compound can save my wife."

George looked at him with an incredulous stare. "Well, this is just a bit much for me. Am I supposed to be influenced by this strange-looking relic?"

"Look closely at it," answered Tony as he held the key closer to George's face. "The two-faced image is Janus, the Roman god of time. In ancient Rome, Janus symbolized change and transitions, such as the progression of the past to the future or the passage from one universe to another. Now, for some reason, this key can reveal specific, future events to certain people, including me. One of those events is the cure of ALS with your drug. The key also revealed that you have an important role in this story; your name was specifically cited in a passage I read over fifty years ago. There is a connection between you, this key, and this crippling disease. Think about it; even your name Janusowski has Janus in it."

At this point, George bristled at Tony's suggestion. "That's ridiculous. You really tell an amusing story, but I must leave now. I have several more meetings lined up for this afternoon, and then I'm joining the Pfizer group at Yankee Stadium this evening to watch an American baseball game. The Yankees are playing their home opener tonight, and I have a lot of work to do before we leave for the game. I do wish the best for your wife, but I can't help you."

As George rose and walked toward the exit, Tony blurted out," Would it change your mind if you knew that you would develop ALS, and your survival will depend on Pol-1905? If you won't give me the compound for my wife's sake, think about your own future."

Tony knew he was interpreting events from the fragmented newspaper article of his youth, but in his last-ditch effort to gain access to Pol-1905, he had no choice but to assume that George Janusowski was the patient who had experienced the miracle cure cited in that headline and play that story off George's emotions. However, instead of responding with concern about his potential fate, George simply shook his head in disbelief and walked away.

CHAPTER THIRTY-TWO

Well, thought Tony, I blew it. In baseball lingo, he had struck out with George Janusowski. But even worse than that, he had sealed Ann's fate. Perhaps he shouldn't have been so truthful with George; the prophecy stories with the key probably scared him off. But what choice did he have? He tried to formulate an alternative plan to approach George. However, his abrupt departure had conveyed an unequivocal message; he had heard enough from Tony. Short of assaulting George and stealing some Pol-1905, there was no way he was going to obtain a sample of the compound. In his desperation, Tony even mulled over this outlandish possibility for a second before dismissing it as sheer lunacy. The only thing to do now was to rush back home to Ann.

As he navigated his way from the hotel onto the gritty and grey streets of Manhattan toward Penn Station, the pent-up stress, frustration, and anxiety of the past few months, a direct result of his single-minded pursuit to uncover a miracle cure for Ann, seemed to erupt all at once in an intense explosion of emotional outbursts. Ensnared in his present, dire situation while investigating strange clues from his past that foretold a future still six years away, he literally felt as if he was chasing time itself. But like navigating a winding river with its many twists and turns, his search had led from one unknown stop to another with no clear destination in sight. Rarely, during his relentless quest, had he paused to vent his own feelings and frustrations. Now they were cascading out of him like a thundering waterfall. He took no notice of his fellow pedestrians, rushing here and there to various locations in the city as he succumbed to his own emotional turmoil. First, he felt extreme rage, railing at fate for dealing him this hand, at George Janusowski for denying him a sample of Pol-1905, and even at himself for failing Ann. Rage surrendered to self-pity. *What more could I have done?* he asked himself. I've literally pursued every lead I could. Finally, his emotions morphed into abject depression as he contemplated life without Ann. Would it even be worth living?

In a zombie-like trance, Tony eventually reached Penn Station, purchased his ticket for the four o'clock train to Wilmington, and joined the long list of passengers forming a snaking queue outside the departure gate. He descended a narrow and dingy staircase to the darkened train platform, entered one of the rail cars marked Coach, and took a window seat. He hardly noticed as the conductor announced the scheduled stops en route to Wilmington: Newark, Newark Airport, Metro Park, Trenton, and Philadelphia, and he barely sensed the movement of the train as it nudged forward out of the station.

Soon the entire train was plunged into the shadows as it entered the century-old rail tunnel that spanned the Hudson River, linking Manhattan to New Jersey. A few minutes later, the train rolled to a complete stop somewhere under the depths of the river. Tony recalled hearing that this ancient tunnel served over four-hundred and fifty trains per day; they were probably delayed yielding the right of way to another passenger train. *How fitting,* he thought. *Stalled in the near-total blackness of a decrepit rail tunnel on the bottom of a river.* The situation perfectly echoed his miserable mood; only darkness lay ahead.

Just then, he noticed a small flicker of shimmering red

light emanating from his jacket pocket. He wouldn't have even detected it except for the eerie black background that permeated the passenger car. His first thought was that the light signaled an incoming message on his phone, but he quickly realized that cell service was non-existent in the subterranean train tunnel. Reaching his hand into his pocket, he pulled out the ancient key and audibly gasped in astonishment as he noticed piercing red lights blazing from one set of Janus's eyes. It was sending him a message!

Tony quickly recovered from the shock of seeing the key light up for him after a fifty-four-year hiatus. His first impulse was to glance around the railcar to observe any unusual movement or activity among his fellow passengers that might signify some sort of signal or message. By now, the train had resumed its journey, and the lighting in the car was markedly improved as it exited the tunnel into the swamplands of northern New Jersey. All the passengers were reclining in their seats, many dozing after a long day of either working or shopping in Manhattan; nothing unusual there. He then grabbed the J.P. Morgan tote bag stashed under his seat and started to comb through its contents. As he was leafing through the conference program booklet, he recalled the message he had read as a boy; it was in the form of a New York Times, front-page headline. Remembering that today's Times was included in his packet of papers, he hastily pulled the newspaper from the bag, unfolded it, and studied the front page. As far as he could tell, no story about the future was referenced in any of the top headlines that included; "North Korea Tests New Weapon," "White House and Justice Department Discuss Congressional Report," and "Democrats Try to Wrest Back Voters."

Just as he was starting to doubt the idea that the paper contained a message, he noted a small insert near the bottom of the page that read, "Yankees Win Home Opener, 8-3." Wait a minute; George Janusowski had told him that the Yankees home opener was tonight. Normally, Tony would have followed the Yankees' schedule religiously and known the specifics of their home opener. However, in his singular quest to help Ann, all extraneous interests, even baseball, had been suspended. Tony quickly turned to Section D of the paper to the sports news. There he read the headline, "Expectations High as Yanks Host Red Sox in Tonight's Home Opener." The ensuing article described the outlook for the Yankees' season and previewed the starting lineup for the night game, scheduled to start at 7:10 p.m. Nowhere did it indicate the game had already been played. According to Tony's watch, the current time was 4:25 p.m. How could the front-page blurb report the score of a game that hadn't occurred yet? This had to be a message from the Janus key!

Tony felt a rush of exhilaration as he pondered his next move. Reaching for his wallet, he pulled out the business card that George Janusowski had handed him only a few hours ago and located his phone number. Entering this number on his iPhone, he texted George the following message. "You want proof? Here it is: Yankees 8 Red Sox 3."

CHAPTER THIRTY-THREE

Upon arriving home later that evening, Tony rushed into the family room to check on Ann. He found her in the same supine position as when he had left her several hours earlier, asleep on her hospital bed. As he approached her sleeping form, he could hear the panting of her labored breathing, so pronounced in the otherwise quiet house. Monica and Andrew joined him and reported that things had been quiet all day; Ann had rarely stirred from her slumber. Probably a result of the benzodiazepines that Dr. Smith had recently prescribed to reduce her anxiety, reasoned Tony; severe drowsiness was a common side effect of her medication. Tony also knew that in the late stage of ALS, patients experience difficulty exhaling the carbon dioxide that promotes drowsiness. This double whammy was probably affecting Ann. *Good,* he thought to himself. *At least she isn't suffering while sleeping.*

As they moved into the kitchen, Monica prodded her father about his day in New York. Looking into his daughter's pleading eyes, Tony decided it was finally time to share his personal story with his children. He replied, "Let me grab a cup of hot tea; then I want to tell you everything." The three of them congregated around the kitchen table, and between sips of the caffeinated beverage, Tony spent the next few hours detailing the entire saga, from his initial discovery of the key as an eighth-grader fifty-four years ago, to its latest message signaling the Yankees win over the Red Sox. Monica and Andrew listened with dumbstruck attention, interrupting periodically with questions but mostly staying quiet during the incredible narrative.

"Show us the newspaper," asked Monica when Tony was finished.

In turn, he pulled the New York Times from his J.P. Morgan tote bag. Scanning the front page, he noticed the small insert that earlier had reported the Yankees score was now gone. "It's not there anymore; just like the headlines from years ago, it disappeared as mysteriously as it had surfaced." He then pulled the key from his pocket and noted it was no longer emitting any light.

"Wait," said Andrew, and he pulled his iPhone from his pocket and started typing in some words. After a few seconds, he read out loud, "Tonight's final score; Yankees 8, Red Sox 3."

"That's just amazing. I can't believe all that you went through to unravel the meaning of that headline. I'm so proud of you," said Monica. "The fact that you found the key again after all these years must mean it's trying to help you, rewarding you for your incredible efforts. What will you do next?"

Tony appreciated his children's unbending faith in him and their positive reaction to his astonishing story. Taking a moment to collect his thoughts, he responded, "It's so late now, past midnight. I suppose I'll call George Janusowski tomorrow morning and ask if the correct score prediction convinced him to provide a sample of the compound." He continued, "Promise me that you won't tell this story to anyone. It just seems like something that's best kept among us. I'm sure you can appreciate that."

Both of them agreed to do so.

The following morning, Tony tried calling George several

times with no success. He also texted George with a message to call back but had no response. George had mentioned that he would be leaving New York today; perhaps he had an early flight, and his cell phone was turned off. However, Tony grew increasingly anxious as the day wore on, and he still hadn't heard from him. Could he have missed him? Or was George choosing to ignore his messages?

At mid-afternoon, while mulling over possible actions, he was interrupted by the chime of the doorbell. Opening the front door, he noticed a FedEx delivery truck parked in front of his house and was greeted by a delivery woman's query.

"Mr. Lucas?"

As he nodded yes, she held out a hand-held tablet displaying a receipt for him to sign. After obtaining his signature, she handed him a small package. Tony thanked her and returned to the kitchen with the package, noticing that the sender's name and address were missing. Carefully opening the box, he observed a small vial containing a white powder and an enclosed note which simply read 83. Attached to the vial was a label stating: 9 grams (90 doses). Nowhere did it indicate the identity of the substance or the name of the sender.

This had to be Pol-1905! Tony's correct prediction of the game score must have convinced George that the prognostic power of the key and the veracity of its message were real. Tony breathed a few silent words of thanks to George, appreciating the risk the pharma executive had taken in circumventing so many of the normal policies that regulated distribution of the compound. The limited information on the package and its contents probably reflected George's efforts to leave as few clues as possible about the true identity of the material or its source.

Tony stared at the vial in disbelief as he weighed the significance of its contents. This material represented the culmination of his single-minded objective over the past several months, ever since Ann's initial diagnosis. Moreover, it represented the potential fulfillment of a prophecy from the newspaper headline he had read over fifty years ago. The countless twists and turns, the many unforgettable characters he encountered along the way, somehow, they had all steered him to this very moment. Thinking back on his odyssey, he recalled the many times the idea of pursuing a cure based on fragmented information he had read as a schoolboy in 1965 seemed both preposterous and hopeless. Somehow he had persevered through all the obstacles and self-doubts. Now was the time to determine if his efforts would pay off. Was Pol-1905 the miracle cure that could save Ann?

CHAPTER THIRTY-FOUR

Knowing that every minute mattered for Ann, Tony rushed to the kitchen and contemplated how to dose the compound. He knew that administering an unapproved drug was against the law; without FDA review, physicians and patients have no way of knowing if a drug is safe and effective. From his earlier research on potential drugs for ALS, he was also aware that there were many unknown factors with this test compound. Would it be degraded to an inactive form by digestive enzymes in the gastrointestinal tract following its administration? Would it be absorbed in appreciable quantities from the gastrointestinal tract into the bloodstream? Would it cross the blood-brain barrier to reach the brain? And even if all those obstacles were overcome, would it actually promote neurogenesis in the brain?

Tony couldn't know the answer to any of these questions; however, in view of Ann's critical condition, he couldn't dwell on these unknowns. This compound represented their very last option, and he had no qualms about administering it to her. Of course, he also knew there were extraordinary and providential circumstances beyond FDA regulations and unknown drug profiles that were driving his decision, namely the events suggested in a newspaper article over fifty years ago that bannered a miracle cure for a crippling disease.

Rereading the label on the vial, he quickly calculated that if the nine grams, or nine thousand milligrams, represented ninety total doses, then each individual dose should be one hundred milligrams. But how to measure one hundred milligrams? Tony had no analytical balance capable of weighing such small amounts. A thought quickly crossed his mind, and he moved to the overhead cabinet where they stored their various pills and supplements. He removed a bottle of Ann's magnesium citrate supplement for bone health and read the label—100 mg gel capsules. Grabbing one of the pills and a small pair of scissors, he returned to his seat at the kitchen table, carefully cut a small slit in the capsule, and emptied the contents onto a paper napkin. There, he thought, that estimates the amount for each dose of the compound. He then fetched a small spatula from his toolbox, sterilized it by running it through several cycles of steaming hot and freezing cold water, and carefully scooped an amount from the vial that approximated the 100 mg of magnesium citrate on the table. He carefully poured the contents into a clean glass, added a small amount of water, and watched the compound rapidly dissolve. Now he was ready to administer the drug solution to Ann.

He drew up the contents of the glass into one of Ann's clean syringes and carried it into the family room, where she was sleeping. His first impulse was to wake Ann and seek her permission before administering the drug. After all, he was planning to dispense an unproven compound that could have unknown, dangerous effects. However, a rapid glance at Ann's cadaverous form reinforced the obvious; she was near death's door. And even if he did rouse her from her benzodiazepine-induced slumber, would she fully comprehend the question of receiving Pol-1905 and the consequences of her decision? He reasoned that he had one, and only one, option. Opening the cap on her feeding tube, he inserted the syringe's tip into the end of the tube and slowly depressed the plunger to deliver the drug. Remembering all the problems he had overcome to reach this point, he breathed a silent, hopeful prayer for the success of this final step in his arduous journey.

Although Tony silently wished for some type of miraculous and immediate reaction from Ann, his left-brain hemisphere, the one responsible for rational thinking, told him otherwise. He had absorbed enough basic pharmacology from his earlier research to appreciate that most drugs' therapeutic effects require multiple dosing, especially in chronic conditions such as ALS. Gazing down at Ann and noting her continued labored breathing only reinforced this concept. He silently committed to repeating this dosing regimen daily until either of two possible outcomes were reached: Ann's recovery or her demise. The real question was, even if Pol-1905 was somehow effective, was the intervention too late for her? All he could do was administer the compound, wait, and pray.

During the next few days, Ann's condition, if anything, seemed to worsen. Her excessive daytime sleepiness, or EDS, that had developed over the past few weeks became even more pronounced, and her breathing became more and more shallow, resulting in severe hypoventilation. Judy, the palliative nurse, explained that this was a state in which reduced amounts of air enter the lungs, resulting in decreased levels of oxygen and increased levels of carbon dioxide in the blood. This gas imbalance promotes a serious increase in the acidity of the blood, termed acidosis, and can severely damage the lungs and kidneys as they struggle to reverse the acidity and raise the pH of the blood. On top of everything else, when Ann was awake, she complained of severe pain throughout her body. In fact, the pain was so excruciating that Judy had started giving her morphine injections.

Through all of this, Ann hung on to precious life. Judy

marveled at her willpower to live. "What a fighter; she won't give in," she remarked to Tony. "It's as if she is holding on by the thinnest of threads in the hope of some last-minute miracle."

In reality, only Tony, Monica, Andrew, and probably George Janusowski knew what this last-minute miracle could possibly be; Pol-1905. Tony had already told his children that he was administering the mysterious compound from the unidentified vial to their mother. And so, he continued his daily ritual of injecting the compound through Ann's feeding tube. However, as the days crept by, he was losing his last shred of hope that Pol-1905 could save her.

CHAPTER THIRTY-FIVE

Tony had adopted the habit of sleeping in the well-worn, leather-upholstered easy chair in the family room to spend as much time as possible with Ann, and on the fourth night since receiving the compound, he assumed his regular position. Sleep had become a very fitful exercise for Tony over the past several months, and as darkness slowly cloaked the entire house, this night proved no exception. Lying awake in the chair for what seemed like an eternity, he estimated the time at 2:30 a.m. and was proven nearly correct with a quick glance at the adjacent clock that glowed 2:31. He remembered playing this same time-guessing game as a student in St. Bridgets when he had first discovered the Janus key. Those days seemed like several lifetimes ago.

Tonight, the only sound that penetrated the darkness was the persistent drip-drip-drip of the leaking tap emerging from the kitchen; it reminded him of the many routine household activities and repairs he had ignored over the past several months. Ann's ALS had certainly turned his life upside down. Suddenly he felt a surge of panic as he realized that one particular sound was missing. During the past few weeks, he had become attuned to the plaintive sound of Ann's shallow breathing. It had provided a constant background noise against the stillness of the night.

However, now, no such noise arose from her bed.

Fearing the worst, he clambered out of the chair and rushed over to check on Ann's condition. He lurched over her shadowy form, grabbed the pale skin of her rail-thin forearm, and pressed his ear down to her chest. Astonishingly, he discerned the gentle, rhythmic sound of soft breathing—no rasping, no wheezing. This was the most peaceful sleep she had experienced in months. *Is this the start of a miracle?* he thought. Could the compound actually be working? Afraid to leave her side for fear of missing any further signs of improvement, he pulled a nearby straight-backed chair next to the bed and spent the rest of the night huddled next to her.

Later that morning, Tony awoke from a fitful sleep and noticed Ann staring up at him with a benevolent smile on her face. "Did you spend the entire night in that chair?" she asked. "Your back must be killing you."

Tony was astounded at the firm tone of her voice. She hadn't been able to pronounce her words so clearly in weeks. He replied, "Don't worry about my back. How are you feeling?"

"I actually feel better than I have in a long time."

Tony could hardly contain his excitement. Her improvement was real! As the morning progressed, positive signs of Ann's recovery were noticeable to everyone in the house, including Judy. "Ann is doing so much better today," she remarked to Tony after using a pulse oximeter clipped to Ann's index finger to estimate the oxygen saturation of her blood. "For the first time in days, her value is over ninety percent. It's as if she has a new lease on life. I can't explain it, but I'm thrilled to see it."

Monica and Andrew were overjoyed at their mother's progress and glanced knowingly in Tony's direction. They understood the real reason behind this miraculous change. Later they cornered their father and spoke in excited tones about prophetic keys and miracle cures. Tony didn't want to jinx any possible recovery and cautioned them to check their enthusiasm. "It really is much too early to assume that your mother will recover; the medical literature is ripe with examples of patients who appear to rally from deadly diseases at the last minute only to succumb shortly thereafter." Inwardly, however, he could barely contain his optimism at the positive developments.

Tony continued the daily regimen of dosing Ann with Pol-1905, and in turn, Ann's extraordinary recovery continued at a remarkable rate. Her breathing and speaking improved each new day, while her systemic pain lessened to the point where she no longer required morphine. Incredibly, she even started walking around the house, slowly and somewhat clumsily, with Tony's support at first, but soon without any aid. Watching her shuffle haltingly from room to room under her own power was a very emotional experience for Tony. He still couldn't believe this was happening.

One afternoon Ann remarked to Tony, "I never thought I'd walk again, and yet here I am getting stronger every day. I know patients aren't supposed to recover from ALS, so there is something special about my case. I have a vague memory of you telling me that your friend, Pietro Rossi, had discovered something important. But everything after that is a complete blank. I'm sure his discovery has something to do with that solution you are giving me each day."

Tony smiled and proceeded to describe in detail the entire story to Ann—Pietro's discovery of George Janusowski; Tony's trip to New York to meet with him and the disappointing outcome; the signal he received from the key about the Yankees score in the bowels of the train tunnel; and finally, the subsequent, covert delivery of the white powder, apparently Pol-1905.

"Your instincts were absolutely correct. You said if the key wanted to get a message to me, it would find a way. Well, it did, and, as a result, you are recovering. I certainly can't explain why or how; perhaps it's a miracle, or perhaps it's just some type of time-bending we'll never understand. But in the end, the only thing that really matters is that you are getting better."

Ann paused for several seconds before responding. "I may have had an intuition about the key, but it was you who made everything happen. You traveled all over to unravel the meaning of that newspaper headline and explored every possible clue. Most importantly, you never gave up on me." Embracing her husband warmly, she continued, "Your love was the real medicine I needed."

A few days later, Ann felt well enough to venture to Dr. Smith's office with Tony for a checkup. As he watched her slow but steady gait en route to the examining room, Dr. Smith marveled at her remarkable transformation. "There is no way you should be walking unaided at this stage of your disease. I have never seen anyone recover so well from late-stage ALS; I can't explain it, so just keep doing whatever you are doing."

After reporting an improvement in all of her vital signs, he had his assistant schedule an appointment for the very next day to remove the feeding tube that had represented the ultimate symbol of Ann's despair. Tony and Ann viewed that happy occurrence as a sure sign that the healing was real.

Some days later, during a follow-up visit to her neurologist, Dr. Gladstone's reaction was much the same. "I want to schedule some more tests to confirm your recovery, but I must admit, standing before me in your current condition is proof that your neurologic functions are improving."

Subsequent results from nerve conduction studies and electromyography confirmed his diagnosis. Dr. Gladstone attributed Ann's recovery to a combination of neurogenesis, the development of new neurons, and neuroplasticity, the ability of the brain to rewire itself by making new neuronal connections. He also suggested that the restoration of Ann's neuronal function would be permanent since whatever trigger had promoted the initial motor neuron destruction was probably long gone from her system. In reality, he couldn't begin to imagine the mysteries that had promoted Ann's recovery and continually expressed his utter amazement at what he had witnessed. "I've never seen anything like this in my thirty-five years of practicing medicine. I'd label it a miracle if I didn't know any better."

In response, Ann's only explanation was to claim that inner strength and external support played the major roles in defeating ALS. For his part, Tony was thrilled that Pol-1905 actually worked for Ann's ALS, despite all the unknown variables with the drug. He had several weeks of doses remaining and intended to administer every last one to Ann.

Over time, a sense of normalcy continued to strengthen its hold on their household. One quiet afternoon, Ann turned to Tony and raised a provocative subject. "Knowing that this compound helped me, don't we have a moral obligation to spread the word for the benefit of other ALS patients? There are literally thousands of people across the globe who know only heartache and despair because of this disease. This drug could completely change so many lives for the better."

Tony carefully considered her question, and after a long reflective pause, responded, "That's a very delicate subject. I violated every FDA regulation in the world to give you the compound, and George violated every legal precedent of his company to send it to me."

"But what about the newspaper headline that mentions a cure for a crippling disease? Doesn't my recovery prove that Pol-1905 is the miracle cure?"

"You're probably right; I've always assumed Pol-1905 is the miracle cure ever since I first heard George describe it in New York. However, that headline refers to an event still in the future, in 2025. We can't go out and proclaim that we know the future; we would be dismissed as lunatics. Also, if we were to announce to the world that Pol-1905 is a miracle cure for ALS, it could create more harm than good. At this point, there are just too many unknowns with this drug. For example, what is its mechanism of action, what is its safety profile, and will it work against different types of ALS? We just don't know. Somehow, we have to convince a pharmaceutical company, whether it be Pol Pharma or another, to begin the normal process for evaluating it as a potential new drug in ALS. If they started that process soon, then by 2025, it could be ready for human use, and the timing would match that of the headline. Let me think about how we can do this."

CHAPTER THIRTY-SIX

As the days rolled on, Ann started to resume many of her pre-ALS activities, at least in a guarded fashion. Dr. Gladstone, although very positive in assessing her outlook, warned that she would be unlikely to recover complete motor function. However, while she certainly wasn't capable of running a marathon or playing a competitive three-set tennis match, she had recovered to the point where, once again, she could start to appreciate the many wonderful experiences that life offered her.

One warm summer afternoon, she turned to Tony and said, "Will you join me for a walk outside?"

As trivial as this request sounded, Tony realized it represented the cusp of another important milestone in her recovery. For up until this moment, her only outdoor ventures were escorted drives to doctor's appointments.

"Of course."

As Tony supported her along a slow amble around the block, he could hardly contain his enthusiasm. "Ann, dear. Do you realize that you are a walking miracle? I couldn't even have imagined this moment just a few weeks ago."

"Well, don't get too excited," she answered with an amused laugh. "I'm not setting any world records here."

Tony read the satisfaction on her face. Suddenly he recalled their first walk together, all those years ago, during the fire alarm episode at Rutgers. He never imagined any walk would stir his emotions as much as that one had. *Shows how much I know,* he thought.

A few days later, Ann achieved another milestone of sorts. The entire family had gathered to celebrate her grandson's sixth birthday. Keyed up by the celebration in his honor, William was currently conspiring with his sister, Emma, and his cousins, Paul and Katie, to wreak havoc on the large Lego castle standing in the center of their family room.

Monica suddenly spoke out, "Dad, we had a question about our IRA contributions and wanted you to review our investment options. Could we do that now on the computer in your office?"

Tony was inwardly pleased that his adult children still turned to him for investment advice. *I guess I did all right over the years, starting with following the advice from Chesley Pritchard after our marriage,* he thought to himself.

As Tony rose to join them, Andrew jumped out of his chair and said. "Mary, we should sit in on this as well. Mom, is it okay if we step out for a few minutes? Will you be all right with the four kids?"

Tony observed a smile forming on Ann's face. For as simple a task as a few minutes of babysitting represented, especially with the parents sitting just a few feet away in another room, this would be her first solo encounter with her beloved grandkids.

Ann responded. "Of course. You five go in the study and do your thing. We'll be fine in here." In fact, Ann's isolation from her grandchildren during the critical stages of her ALS had been one of her greatest regrets.

About twenty minutes later, Tony joined the adults as they returned to the family room. He smiled broadly upon observing the four kids nestled on the sofa around their beloved nana, who was reading them the classic childhood story, Alexander and the Terrible, Horrible, No Good, Very Bad Day.

Yes, he thought one more time, *miracles do happen.*

One afternoon, Tony surprised Ann by stating, "Let's take a ride." Escorting her to their car, he drove to downtown Wilmington and parked on one of the side streets off the main thoroughfare. Assisting her out of the car, they slowly walked several hundred feet until they came to one storefront with large lettering stating, ROSA'S MEAL SERVICE.

"Rosa was instrumental in helping me discover the secret of Almedinilla," he told Ann, "and I promised to share any information I discovered about her father. She is also anxious to meet you in person."

They went inside and were warmly greeted by Rosa, who escorted them back to her office, where a tray of Italian biscotti almond cookies and a pot of hot tea were waiting. Over the refreshments, Tony proceeded to tell her what he had learned about Robert Arbore's trip to Italy and Spain all those years ago, emphasizing Robert's experience with the glowing key that had steered both Pietro Rossi and him to Almedinilla. When finished, he pulled the key out of his pocket and handed it to Rosa for inspection.

"Pietro was kind enough to give it to me in Almedinilla, and it led me to the drug that promoted Ann's miraculous recovery, just as it successfully guided your father to a new source of olive oil. As I mentioned during our earlier visit, I had a notion that there was a special connection between your father and me ever since we met at the Orioles baseball game in 1983, and this key proved to be the common link."

Rosa examined the key carefully before returning it to Tony. "It certainly is exquisitely sculptured," she replied. "The Janus figurine appears so life-like. Thank you for sharing this miraculous story with me about this unknown chapter in my father's life. I always knew he had a special gift. We used to refer to it as his obsession with time, and it must have been this talent that enabled him to interpret the message from the key just as you were able to decipher your own messages. What an incredible saga. I can only wonder what miracles this key has in store for others who may fall under its influence."As Tony and Ann stood to depart. Rosa asked, "Why do you think olive oil played such a crucial role in all the stories? As you mentioned, it represented another common element for you, my father, and the Roman merchant?"

Tony had actually given this question considerable thought but could never really come up with a satisfactory answer. "I really don't know," he responded. "One possibility is that both the olive oil and the metals from which the bronze key was forged, tin and copper, originated from Iberia. I know that ancient Rome procured many of their metals for jewelry and weapons from Iberia, just as they did their olive oil. Perhaps a common origin may have something to do with the recurring connections between the key and the olive in all of our stories. I suppose we'll never know for sure."

With those words, Rosa stood, warmly embraced both of them, and wished them continued good health as they exited her office.

CHAPTER THIRTY-SEVEN

A few weeks later, Tony surprised Ann with a question." Do you feel well enough to take a trip to Spain?"

Ann was feeling much stronger and readily answered yes. In fact, she was anxious to visit Almedinilla and meet Pietro; both had played such an important role in her recovery. Tony made all the travel arrangements, and the following week they departed for Spain using the same Philadelphia to Madrid to Granada route he had used earlier. Driving through the beautiful Andalusian landscape, Tony recalled his earlier hope that one day he could share this experience with Ann. How implausible that wish had seemed a few months ago, yet here they were fulfilling Ann's lifelong wish to visit Spain. Amazing!

Arriving in Almedinilla, they checked into the same charming hotel that Tony had stayed in earlier. Unpacking his suitcase, he told Ann, "I thought you should rest for a while, and then if you feel up to it, we can explore part of the city."

Although Ann was captivated by the enchanting town and anxious to explore its picture-book streets, she actually was exhausted from her trip and agreed with Tony's suggestion. As she succumbed to her weariness, Tony had to remind himself that she was still recovering from a severe neurological disease. Tourist activities could definitely wait. In fact, Ann slept soundly for the rest of the afternoon and through that night.

The following morning, Tony escorted Ann to a small cafe near the hotel for breakfast. "There is someone here that I know you will want to meet," he told her upon entering the small cafe. As they approached one of the tables, a well-dressed, elderly man of average height stood and greeted them. Tony immediately moved toward the man and warmly embraced him in a gentle bear hug. "Ann," he said, "I'd like to introduce you to my good friend, Pietro Rossi."

Ann greeted Pietro with a hug as she spoke. "I can't thank you enough for everything you have done for us. Without your help, I wouldn't be standing here today."

"I am so pleased that, in some small way, my efforts have helped to make this happy reunion possible."

Over a breakfast of bollos, or buns, toast with olive oil, and cafe con leche, Tony updated Pietro on his recent activities, including meeting with George Janusowski in New York, unraveling the signal from the glowing key in the train tunnel, and eventually receiving the test compound that promoted Ann's miraculous recovery.

Pietro could only nod in astonishment at the amazing story and replied, "I knew that returning the key to you was the correct thing to do. I'm so pleased it enabled you to discover the miracle cure mentioned in that mysterious newspaper headline from your youth and helped your beautiful wife recover. As I said before, you were meant to have it."

Tony then took a small box from his pocket and presented it to Pietro. "I know we can never repay you for all that you have done, but please accept this small memento as a reminder of our enduring gratitude towards you."

Pietro took the box and opened it to reveal a pocket watch sporting a fourteen-inch metal chain. The bronze cover, engraved with the image of an olive tree, opened up to reveal Roman numerals and classic black hands on the watch face. On the back was an engraving that read, To Pietro, our dear friend. We will never forget. Tony and Ann.

Moved by this gracious display of affection, Pietro answered, "It's perfect, a timepiece with an olive tree on its cover. Did you know that, according to legend, the founders of Rome, the brothers Romulus and Remus, were born in the shade of an olive tree? Over the ages, olive oil has become both a cultural and religious symbol and, of course, an emblem for peace. And now, because of your story, the oil from the olive tree has come to represent a dimension of time that has mysteriously linked the lives of total strangers. What gift could be more appropriate? I assure you I will never forget you or this amazing saga. Thank you."

Shortly thereafter, Tony and Ann bid Pietro a warm farewell and, promising to stay in touch, left the cafe.

Tony spent the rest of the morning as a tour guide escorting Ann around the rustic streets of Almedinilla. They maintained a leisurely pace, stopping often to rest and enjoy the charm of the old-world town with its picturesque collection of whitewashed homes and shops. It was a beautiful, sunny day, and Tony still couldn't believe he was sharing this experience with Ann; just a few weeks ago, she had lain on death's very doorsteps. His thoughts then turned to Ann's real savior, George Janusowski. During the past few weeks, Tony had left several messages for George, informing him of their trip to Almedinilla in hopes of arranging a meeting. They still had so much to discuss. He reasoned that George was a frequent visitor to Spain since his fiancée, Dolores Vidal, lived there. But as of yet, George had not returned his messages.

Soon Ann began to tire from her excursions, and they made their way back to the hotel where she spent most of the afternoon resting. When she awoke several hours later, Tony surprised her with news that George had texted him back and asked them to meet him for dinner at one of Almedinilla's famous tapas restaurants.

"That sounds wonderful!" said Ann. "It should be a very interesting evening."

Tony and Ann arrived at the restaurant at eight and found it buzzing with activity that reflected its popularity among the citizens and tourists of Almedinilla. Tapas are staples of Spanish cuisine that consist of small portions of different foods, including breads, meats, sautéed vegetables, or other tasty morsels.

Scanning the restaurant for George and failing to spot him, they took a table to await his arrival. Within a few minutes, Tony spotted George approaching. Rising to greet him, Tony said, "I'm so glad we could meet again. I owe you so much, and there are some important matters I want to discuss with you." He then introduced George to Ann, who thanked him profusely for providing the compound that had saved her life.

Tentatively, George mumbled, "You're welcome; I'm glad it helped you." Tony sensed that George was extremely uncomfortable about this meeting, and George's next words confirmed Tony's suspicions. "I must admit I was hesitant to meet with you again. I had a lot of explaining to do when our partner company discovered the amount of the test compound specified by our MTA was nine grams short. I violated too many company regulations to count in forwarding that sample to you. It probably is best if I just put the whole affair behind me."

"You can't do that," answered Tony. "Ann's miraculous recovery is proof that there is something special about Pol-1905. We have to figure out a way to advance its development as a treatment for ALS; think of the potential benefit for thousands of patients."

George mulled over Tony's comments for several seconds before replying. "Even if I wanted to promote its development as an ALS treatment, there is no practical way I can do that. First of all, neither of us can admit what we have done; me sending you a sample of the compound or you administering it to your wife. If either of us were to come out and claim we have proof Pol-1905 works in an ALS patient, we would be subject to a criminal investigation. And beyond that, Pol Pharma's in-house expertise is built around arthritis, not CNS. We have no internal capabilities or competencies to develop Pol-1905 as a drug for ALS; the preclinical experiments and the clinical programs are completely different for the two therapeutic areas. And finally, even if I could convince Pol Pharma's board that the compound has potential benefit in ALS, developing it for that indication would conflict with our arthritis program. Competition for all developmental resources, including financial, facility, and personnel, would critically impair both programs. Pol Pharma is a small company with limited resources, and by necessity, we have to abide by the one drug one one disease practice, even if it seems inefficient."

Tony thought carefully before answering. "Your arguments are completely rational and applicable for normal situations. But this is anything but a normal situation. Look at what we know and how we discovered that information. That key was sending me—no, sending us—a message, and the Yankees-Red Sox score prediction, followed by Ann's amazing recovery, is proof of its veracity. In light of what we know, don't we have a moral obligation to follow-up with Pol-1905?"

George looked at Tony and responded, "Ah, yes, this is what I was afraid of. You are a very persuasive individual. When we first met in New York, there was something about you that made me take you seriously, even with your crazy story of futuristic newspaper headlines and magic keys. That's part of the reason why I almost opted to forgo this meeting with you. Still, I cannot agree to your suggestion; there are just too many hurdles to overcome."

"But what about your own future?" Ann interjected as she joined the discussion. "You didn't see me before Pol-1905 arrived, but I assure you it was not a pretty picture. I was literally on death's doorstep. Now, look at me, touring Spain and eating tapas. Late-stage ALS patients are not supposed to recover like this. According to Tony's newspaper article from 1965, six years from now, a miracle cure will probably be reported for this very disease. And the article mentioned you by name. Since you are not a physician or the inventor of the drug, it's possible that you will be an ALS patient responding to the miracle cure. You may need this compound developed for ALS. Your very life may depend on it."

George considered these words and replied, "You may be correct; I have an uncle who died of ALS, so there is a history in my family. However, I still don't see how I can publicize it to other companies without jeopardizing all of us."

Tony then added, "I may be able to help alleviate some of your concerns. I have a contact at a pharmaceutical company that specializes in developing CNS drugs. In fact, they have an ongoing discovery program for ALS. I could inform him that I learned Pol-1905 affects neurogenesis without revealing any names or specifics. With that information, this company may very well have an interest in learning more and testing a sample in their own labs. Perhaps then a mutually beneficial partnership could be established, granting them the right to develop Pol-1905 as an ALS treatment while Pol Pharma continues its development for arthritis. I'm no expert, but I know that sometimes multiple indications are pursued for a single compound."

George responded, "You've definitely done your homework in trying to convince me. In certain cases, most commonly with cancer drugs, compounds are developed simultaneously for multiple indications, although usually, the compound is assigned a different name for each program to avoid confusion among the various stakeholders. Your arguments are compelling, especially if ALS is in my future, although that is something I don't want to dwell on. Why don't you speak with your contact and, if he is amenable, put him in touch with me? You might suggest that an academic scientist in a remote Polish University got hold of the compound and discovered it promoted neurogenesis. However, this scientist is bound by a confidentiality agreement not to reveal his data. Perhaps this story would convince your contact, and we'll see what develops."

Tony and Ann nodded in agreement. Apparently, the possibility that George could develop ALS had helped convince him to pursue this course of action. For Tony and Ann, this was the best outcome they could have hoped for.

As they chatted over their tapas dinner, Tony provided more details about his experiences with the Janus key and the trail of events that led him to seek out George in New York. Tony then added, "I'm really sorry for lying about knowing Dolores, but I had no options left. As it turned out, if the key hadn't revealed the Yankees score to me, none of this would be happening."

"Why me?" asked George. "Why am I involved in your story? I have no known connection with either of you or with any ancient Roman relic."

"I can't answer that, but perhaps your connection with the olive trees from Spain and the products derived from its leaves may be the answer. That is one of the common themes in all the stories. We may never know for sure. However, it appears that my role in this story is almost finished; the next chapter is in your hands."

Promising to stay in touch, George bid farewell to Tony and Ann and departed the restaurant.

Tony and Ann spent the next few days touring the Andalusian region of Spain before returning home. After the brutal months they had both endured since Ann's initial diagnosis, their short respite through the beautiful southern region of Spain seemed like a second honeymoon. During their travels, Tony was particularly interested in learning as much as possible about the traditions and legends of the olive tree and its oil in hopes of trying to make some sense of why this commodity represented a common link with all the players in the improbable tale. As Pietro had mentioned, the olive tree has long been held as a symbol of many virtuous characteristics, including victory, longevity, perseverance, justice, fertility, wisdom, and others. The famous Greek poet Homer referred to it as "liquid gold." The Roman poet Virgil used the olive branch as a symbol of peace in his Aeneid. Because of its ability to survive droughts and germinate in hard, rocky soil inhospitable to most plants, oil from the olive tree was believed to bestow strength and health on those who consumed it. Perhaps, in the final analysis, these universal metaphors for olive oil were all that were necessary to understand why this humble commodity had united so many diverse characters.

CHAPTER THIRTY-EIGHT

Three Months Later

Tony scanned the business section of his daily newspaper and caught sight of one story that captured his attention. "Look at this," he said to Ann, who was sipping hot tea across the table from him. The headline read, "Local Pharma Company Inks Deal with Polish Start-Up." The article described how Hopeton Pharmaceuticals of Philadelphia entered into an agreement with Pol Pharma, based in Warsaw, Poland, to develop one of the latter company's proprietary molecules for CNS diseases, including ALS.

"Looks like your discussions with Jim Cahill paid off," she noted.

"Jim is such a good guy. He suspected I wasn't telling him the complete story about Pol-1905 promoting neurogenesis, but he was sufficiently intrigued to speak with George and eventually confirm its activity in their own in-house assays. With the development program underway, if all goes well, the compound should be ready for use in ALS patients by the time the newspaper article mentioning George Janusowski appears in six years or so. In any case, that's good news for George. If, in fact, he is an ALS patient who needs a miracle cure, the drug will be a godsend for him. And even if he isn't a victim of ALS, the success of the compound will be a boon, both for him and his company. I guess we'll just have to wait and see which scenario plays out."

"I just keep thinking," remarked Ann, "how can this key forecast the future?"

Tony had spent endless days thinking about that very question but offered no concrete answer. "I'm pretty sure we will never know," he replied. "Physicists and philosophers still debate different theories of time. Some have even proposed that what we know as time is not real but rather an illusion made up of human memories and experiences. If that is so, then perhaps the reality is that the past, present, and future all exist at once. I certainly can't grasp such a concept, but somehow, the key may have altered my notion of time and given me a view into the future. Why it chose me, Lucius Antonius, and Robert Arbore, I can't know for sure, except that we all apparently had some special aptitude for time. Perhaps this intuition was the requirement that allowed the three of us to view a glimpse of the future. The olive oil represented an additional link that joined the three of us. And for me, the Yankees' references kept on appearing. In the final analysis, all that really matters is that my view into the future provided the solution to keep us together."

"That's good enough for me," Ann nodded in agreement. "We've been given a gift, and I don't intend to question it."

Tony added, "There's one more thing; it's something that Rosa said. Remember, she could only wonder what this key has in store for others who may fall under its influence. I can't believe its powers end here. But as long as I keep it, it can never reveal itself to anyone else. The key has fulfilled its prophecy for me; now, I believe it is time to let it discover other folks with an obsession with time. Let it help them; it's really not mine to keep anymore."

"What do you propose?"

"Well, if I donated it to a museum, it would be guarded day and night, so that's not an option. I think the best solution might be to place it in an antique shop where it would be on display to capture the interest of potential buyers. That's how Pietro discovered it, and we know how that turned out. I think I'll find a suitable shop and donate it to them."

"Sounds good. Now we better get organized; we promised to take the grandkids to the zoo today."

Tony smiled. For now, a pleasant afternoon with his wife and grandkids was as far into the future as he needed to see.

Thomas Reilly is a retired Pharmaceutical and Biotechnology scientist with an expertise in drug discovery and development. He holds a doctoral degree in microbiology. He has been writing essays and articles on science and technology for years. CHASING TIME is his first novel. He lives in Wilmington, Delaware, with his wife, Linda.

Made in the USA
Middletown, DE
04 August 2022

70550396R00128